Before I Died

by

Sara Marx

Bella
BOOKS

2011

Bella Books, Inc.
P.O. Box 10543
Tallahassee, FL 32302

Printed in the United States of America on acid-free paper.

First Bella Books Edition 2011

Edited by Katherine V. Forrest
Cover designed by Judith Fellows

ISBN: 13 978-1-59493-250-2

Other books by Sara Marx

InSight of the Seer
Decoded

To Macy, Christian, Mary and Roxy (of course).
To You.

About the Author

Sara Marx lives on a Florida beach with her partner, Mary. They are parents to a brood that include two political/peace activists, an actor and a United States presidential candidate for 2044.

Acknowledgements

Thank you to my dear editor, Katherine V. Forrest, for your never-ending patience and beautiful guidance. You kindly teased apart my mangled grammar and lopsided structure and performed every necessary chore to get the story on track and keep it there. It is an absolute privilege to work with you. Thanks for this book and the last one, too. The next one, too. I'll see you in the cue.

Thank you, Ruth Stanley, proofreader extraordinaire and mathematician. You (slide) rule.

Thank you to my parents, who taught me and my sister about recycling and keeping the earth clean long before it was en vogue. They continue to exemplify responsibility to this planet, from composting to recycling. What a fun and considerate home to spring from.

Thank you to Macy and Christian, my best assistants. You're both quick with a line, a name or a joke—whatever it takes to keep me sane. I appreciate it and I love you.

Thank you to Roxy and her nutty narrator who do absolutely nothing to keep me sane, but are always good for a few laughs. I love our situation.

Thank you, Teri Maher, my first set of eyes, and Linda for telling me to write this down.

Thank you Karin Kallmaker. Can I say again how glad I am that we're finally working together? I am.

Before I Died is peppered with references to Riverkeeper, a watchdog organization whose members and volunteers work tirelessly to keep the Hudson River free of pollution and protect drinking water for more than nine million New York residents. To learn more about the organization, please visit www.Riverkeeper.org.

It's my pleasure to surround myself with people who are much smarter than I am. The information in this book came to me by way of reliable individuals and from watching too much network news. This novel contains my interpretation of those stories, and any inaccuracies are strictly my own.

I'm a great fan of this lovely planet and I realize how important it is to try to do right by Her. I'm far from perfect, but I am a good tryer. This book is for the other tryers who regard Mother Nature with much tenderness and love. You are wonderful.

Chapter 1

"I am dead."

"What makes you say that, Laney?"

"Because I see snow, wind blowing trees and the frozen pond below, yet I don't feel cold."

"What do you feel?"

The low, thickly-accented voice sounded from behind me, but I didn't seek out its owner just yet. I was still taking inventory of my senses, well aware of everything I should be feeling. Icy blasts of wind coming off the water should have been searing my lungs, squeezing misty, gasping breaths from my lips, evidence of a brand of northern cold I was quite familiar with.

"Nothing. I feel nothing." My shoulders sank slightly. I stopped walking and turned to see my companion, but no one was there. I closed my eyes, breathed deeply, tried hard to feel anything and even harder to put what I did feel into words.

"The air around me is warm. It's…balmy."

I opened my eyes and looked down, wondering where my shoes were. Snowflakes gently dusted my bare feet and jaggedly flitted along the ice-laden pathway, ducking inside frosty caverns until the wind swept them out again. The path should have felt bumpy, freezing—*anything*, but not nothing.

I leaned over the railing and looked down to discover that the bridge did not span a lake, but a river. I was struck with familiarity. "I know this place."

"Do you now?"

I raised my eyes, peered out through a web of windswept auburn hair, mystified that I didn't even find it necessary to squint against the blindingly white winter sky. I motioned toward the horizon. "There's a high school that direction about a mile and beyond it is my childhood home. I used to cross this bridge every day."

"Indeed you did."

My memories gained greater dimension with each passing millisecond. My head felt clear and trouble-free. Questions formed too rapidly to ask and I failed in my attempt to streamline them in order of importance. Instead, I went with the most obvious first.

"Who are you?" I turned in a semicircle and tried without success to locate my companion. "And why are we here?"

"It's better than coming through alone. You have questions."

I spoke to the wind. "Do you have answers to my questions?"

"No. You do."

Two adults made their approach, bundled in long wool coats and hunting-style hats, flaps down, their hands chucked deep into pockets. Thick scarves whipped around in gale force winds and they appeared to look right through me. One scarf unwound itself from its owner's neck and floated toward me. It was graceful, like a banner on parade day. He started to double back and make a lunge for it, but was stopped by his fellow traveler.

"Leave it. It's too cold to go chasing nonsense."

I imagine this was probably easier said by the fellow whose scarf remained swaddled tightly around his neck. The other hiked up the collar of his coat and the pair forged ahead, nearly crashing into me. With more spryness than I could have possibly anticipated, I jumped out of the way and nearly fell into my companion. That's how I got my first look at him.

He stood beside me like a tower, in slacks and a dark turtleneck, looking every bit the part of a magazine model. I studied his beautiful face, flawless cocoa skin and smooth head, his thin aquiline nose and golden and almost troubled-looking eyes. I felt no trouble at all, only a little confusion over what had just occurred.

"Those men could not see us."

"They could not," he acknowledged.

"Are we…ghosts?" I stammered the absurd question, but it was no more absurd than me standing on a bridge in the middle of winter wearing no shoes. I glanced ahead at the men who were nearly out of sight by now. "Would they have walked through us had we not moved?"

"It's not like that," my companion answered in his silky, smooth voice. His smile was brilliant, but fleeting. "They would have merely bumped into you and wondered what tricks their minds were playing. Most likely they'd end up blaming their imaginations."

"You said me. What if they'd bumped into you?"

His look bordered on sly and he shook his head. "I'm wise enough to get out of the way."

He started to walk again in his long strides and I hurried to catch up. By now, I'd surmised it was evening—a dreary one at that—and that the town was as quiet and dull as it had been in my memory. An occasional car would pass, each winding those frozen flurries into one dizzying multidimensional tornado after another. My senses were refining at warp speed. I'd never been so acutely aware of every aspect of the bridge—every crack, crater and nick in the concrete side walls. Mesmerized by these details, it seemed to me like we'd been walking forever by the time the structure began its descent.

Up ahead, I saw the lost scarf trapped against the chain-link fence that ran the length of the bridge. It was high up there, held hostage by an angry wind. A small girl no more than eight moved toward us. She wore only a thin sweater and tights that looked like they'd been the sole support for a family of moths. Her toes poked through the ends of her shoes and the skin of her sweet brown face was chapped and sallow looking. Deep-set wide eyes were underscored with dark shadows and were locked on mine as she came closer.

"She sees us," I said.

"Yes."

"Is she dead, too?"

"Not yet."

I hurriedly poked my bare toes through the chain links, I rescued the scarf and with unfathomable litheness and speed, leapt down. The chain links against my bare feet had not hurt at all, nor had my rough landing. The child walked directly to me and I wound the scarf around her neck several times. It was three times as long as she was tall, and its wide tails draped her emaciated body like a second sweater when I finished. She hugged me tightly and I held her for a while, slightly puzzled at myself for not feeling extremely sad about her obvious poverty. I instead felt effervescent with a strange peacefulness, though I am not sure why since my companion hinted that the child might not be on this earth for much longer. At last I released her and she passed us and continued on her journey.

"Am I an angel?" I asked, still basking in the afterglow of the gentle hug. I did not want to ask too much about dying children just yet.

"Not even close."

I should have been disappointed, yet I remained surprisingly even-tempered. The hug was wearing off, but I still remembered its good feeling. "I would be a terrific angel."

"Would you now?" My companion's voice sounded like it was smiling.

I suddenly remembered that I was wearing a jacket. The jacket that went with my black pants and new shoes—the one I'd put on before...

"Wait, call to her!" I touched my lapels, felt the softness of the sheepskin. "I'll give her my jacket. Whatever I am, I no longer need it."

I started to remove the jacket, but my companion reached out and stopped me. His eyes narrowed in a cautionary gaze as he looked me up and down. For the first time I examined my tattered and singed clothes. The shredded remains of my jacket would be useless for warmth or comfort. I closed my eyes tight as white light flashed against black in my mind's eye. I heard the dreadful screeching sound of an engine descending too rapidly. I heard the sharp intake of my own breath.

My eyelids rapidly fluttered wide open. My companion seemed already aware of my eventual reaction and his face showed true compassion. "That is why I am here."

"I'm not in heaven."

He shook his head.

From our place on the bridge, I surveyed the fledgling town wrapped in a blanket of frozen mist. The Iowa town looked every bit as miserable as I'd remembered. "Is Willow Creek hell?"

He wore a hint of a know-it-all expression. "You always thought it was, didn't you?"

"God Almighty. I don't want to burn for all eternity in Willow Creek." My desire for answers was not as strong as it surely should have been, odd, given that I was hazy on the details of…everything. Notions of my lover and our children wound through my head with an electrifying force, becoming clearer with each passing second. I blinked hard, asked, "Where are Mara and my children?"

His steely gaze eclipsed my fear, making it impossible to launch into full-scale panic.

My voice dropped to a whisper. "Why am I here?"

"Because we have someplace to be," he answered. "Hurry."

Chapter 2

I followed my companion under the bridge to an old brick warehouse that had been converted into a restaurant long ago. It had been *Vito's Little Italy* when I was young. Now it was *Jimmy's, a Multicultural Cuisine Experience!* according to the flashing sign posted out front. I wondered if this was where we had to be.

The smell of grease and steaks hung heavily in the air around the restaurant, but did not inspire even an inkling of a hunger pang from me. As we walked inside, I instantly missed the blast of steamy warmth that normally greets one upon entering any restaurant from the stark Iowa winter.

The inside was bustling with patrons, but was much different than the atmosphere I remembered where waiters and bus boys called to each other in Italian. Those staff members were gone, replaced with Spanish-speaking busers and college students in jeans who were waiting tables.

People walked past us, nearly stepped on us, but I was getting quick on my feet without all that much practice. A young Latina wearing tight black jeans and a low-cut blouse leaned her voluptuous figure against a podium near the entrance. She talked on her cell phone, oblivious to our presence.

An older gentleman came bustling down a long hallway. His hair was wiry and gray and his mustache had been waxed into perfect upturned curls. He showered my companion with salutations one reserves for an old friend and didn't seem at all taken aback by my appearance or ruined clothing. In Italian, he asked my companion who I was. I surprised him by answering him in his language—albeit amateurish and somewhat disjointed. He told me his name was Vito and then he smiled and clasped my hand, and instantly I knew that our touch was of the same nothingness.

I looked at my companion without asking the question that was obviously front and center in my brain. He nodded his confirmation that our fine host was also dead.

Vito invited us to follow him, and we weaved through the crowded restaurant until he seated us near the kitchen.

"The best seats in the house!" he bragged. "Nice and comfy warm!"

I figured we all knew that it didn't matter if it was warm or not. My companion requested that Vito tell us about the specials and the odd fellow graciously complied, reciting them in flowery Italian detail. We told him our selections and Vito grinned, the ends of his old-world mustache practically tickling his squinted eyes. He left, and I figured it was time to have something besides "companion" to call my companion.

"Who are you?"

"Trinidad Anwar."

"You live—*lived* here?" I quickly corrected myself.

"No. Bangladesh."

I slowly nodded. "That would explain your accent."

"Bengali."

"Okay," I said. His words tickled a gentle memory in the far recesses of my mind, but I pushed the thought aside, focused on my quest to discover exactly what I'd become. "And now you live…?"

He only smiled. I rubbed my temples, though I felt no headache.

"So let me see if I get this—some of the patrons here are living and others are dead?"

He nodded. I watched the flurry of wait staff activity, some dressed in old-world attire and others in designer jeans and T-shirts. It seemed to be simply a difference of wardrobe that set the dead apart from the living. That and the odd sense of camaraderie the dead seemed to have with one another evidenced by how their eyes would meet and twinkle, as if they shared a secret.

Two young men were engaged in a spat over a broken plate. As they carried on, I studied the subject of the debacle and realized the ceramic plate shards were old, very different from the modern glass platters the living were eating from. None of the living had noticed the smashing sound the plate had made when it hit the floor, nor did they hear the boys' escalating volume, despite that many living were being seated very near the incident. I already knew, but I asked anyway. "Those boys, they are also dead?"

"Yes."

"And Vito is the original owner of this place." It was slowly coming together.

"He was once upon a time. And please don't remind him about the new sign outside. It makes him very angry," he said, taking a sip from his water. When he finished, he raised the glass and looked at it with a thoughtful expression. "Delicious."

"Is it?" I touched my glass, which was the same tepid temperature as everything else around me. I took a sip and narrowed my eyes. I took another. Disappointed, I set my glass aside. "It tastes like nothing."

Trinidad lowered his voice. "I recommend that you do not make that same remark about our food when it arrives unless you want to create a scene. Vito takes his craft very seriously."

I might have laughed at the notion of offending dead people had I not felt so inexplicably content.

In my childhood, my grandmother told me stories about sharing wine and bread with Vito and his wife at this very restaurant. I wondered if the old fellow would remember my dear Gran Eleanor, but I decided not to bring it up. There were too many important things to talk about with Trinidad. I didn't want to waste unnecessary time making polite conversation with Vito.

I watched the dead waiters gracefully dodge the living ones, and listened to an array of colorful swears in English, Spanish, and Italian expelled from the kitchen with each swoosh of the old metal door. When Vito finally reemerged, he carried two heaping plates that he proudly set before us. He shouted something—my Italian is quite limited—and soon a young boy came along with bread and grated parmesan cheese, which he liberally sprinkled over our pasta. Dead or alive, it looked delicious.

Trinidad poised his fork over the mountain of fettuccini and glanced over at me. As Vito was anxiously watching us, and as I knew Trinidad's look bore a warning that I should behave, we simultaneously twirled our forks, winding pasta around the tines. We then took our first bites. I chewed the pasta thoughtfully and considered that with their texture as the only basis by which to judge, it was everything that I imagined chewing a plate of soggy rubber bands would be like. Trinidad's smiling eyes were still on me. I forced myself to swallow, then I smiled.

"It's absolutely delectable," I told Vito.

Thrilled with my review, he began to sing an Italian song I'd heard my grandmother sing when I was a child. He left our table, his vibrato growing stronger, echoing off the walls of the narrow hallway leading to the kitchen. Once he'd pushed through the swinging door, the singing promptly ceased and again we heard Vito barking orders at the dead cook staff. I gazed over at the other diners who were oblivious to it. Only the dead patrons had heard the dead man's serenade.

Trinidad continued to eat, but I could no longer remain quiet. "How can they all work here together—the dead and the living?"

"Just as you see them do it."

"And many dead patrons dine here on food with no taste?"

Trinidad began to twirl his fork again. "For some people, this place is heaven. For Vito it certainly is. It's different for everyone. Their loving memories are powerful enough to subsidize anything they may lack."

"It seems to me that for the chef, the diners' inability to taste their food would be the ultimate punishment."

Trinidad looked at me, the corners of his mouth slightly upturned. "And in the case of certain chefs, perhaps it is the ultimate blessing for the diners."

I shrugged. "Why am I here?"

"To better absorb your circumstances before we continue."

I watched Trinidad take his third bite. I couldn't see the point, but I began to twirl the pasta again, a smaller amount this time. As I took the bite, I tried to remember how fettuccini tasted the way Eleanor made it on Sundays long ago. It made my effort a little more palatable, but I can't say it was delicious.

"Why eat if I can't taste it?" I asked.

"The good news is you won't gain weight."

It was really the last thing on my mind.

I whispered, "Do they know they're *dead?*"

"Yes, though some have forgotten by now." He blotted the sauce from his lips and took another sip of water, all actions that were pointless as far as I was concerned.

"Do they go home at night? Do they have places to live?"

"They live where they were their happiest."

I lowered my gaze, but my eyebrow arched. "You're not telling me that this town is heaven, because I beg to differ."

"For some it is heaven."

We were silent.

"I was just wondering if you could be any vaguer?"

He ignored my question, politely folded his napkin and laid it before him on the table. Vito received his signal and was back at our table reciting the dessert menu. I started to refuse, but Trinidad cut me off and ordered biscotti and espressos, which was enough to send Vito practically skipping off to the kitchen.

I leaned across the table and spoke quietly. "What's the point?"

"To leave without enjoying dessert would be rude. Vito lives to serve his people."

I stared at him. "Do you think that's an entirely accurate statement?"

Vito was back with the espressos, almond biscuits and dessert, which had not been my favorite when I'd been amongst the living. I figured that without the benefit of taste, I might actually like them better this time around. We nibbled and sipped and made polite conversation with the dead restaurant owner until it was time to go. Vito proclaimed us to be good friends of the establishment and said that our food was on the house. But of course.

I smiled as the old man planted kisses on our cheeks and I wished him well. We weaved around tables, successfully avoiding the harried wait staff as we made our way to the door. Between the living and the dead, the place was packed. My thoughts were somewhere else at the moment, in a small apartment in New York, where my heart belonged.

I needed to ask Trinidad about her—about them...

The sudden appearance of the only other woman in my life dispelled my intended inquiry and—pardon the pun—stopped me dead in my tracks.

Chapter 3

Mama was seated at a tiny table for two in the crowded restaurant.

In another time, there would have been ten or twelve relatives bordering two tables pushed together, heaping bowls of pasta and sauce down the middle, wine and laughter both freely flowing. Tonight she was alone and looking sadder than any living person in the restaurant.

Remarkably, I noticed that my mother looked a lot like me, only her hair was shorter and she had more lines around her mouth and eyes. I remember when her auburn hair was as long as mine and how she would wear it pulled back in two antique tortoiseshell combs that I could never see tucked deep in her mane, but I knew they were there. She'd show them to me at night after she'd let her hair down to breathe. Now, free from the weight of those long tresses, her hair lay in springier curls around her shoulders and created a gentle frame around her unusually pale face. I'd never seen it so short. It was nice.

She sipped a glass of wine and stared at the plate of something in front of her that looked like it had come from a can and decorated with an oversized sprig of parsley. It was far less appetizing than what we'd been served, the whole no-taste issue notwithstanding. I wondered if Vito was put off by the lackluster plates that rolled off the line for the living patrons.

Though I had not visited my hometown in eight years, I didn't see a face I knew other than Mama's. There was nobody to comfort her or even stop by her table to greet her. I felt sorrier than ever for her. As my father hated dining out, I knew Mama would sometimes go alone, which she did not like. She'd complained about this very thing only recently during our weekly phone call. Or at least I thought it was only last week...

She looked tiny, much thinner than I remembered her, and I would have given anything to have sat right down with her and ordered up a bottle of house red.

Trinidad did not stop me when I approached her. I stopped a few feet away from her and watched as she traced the top of her wineglass with her index finger, eyes unmoving and trance-like. Her nose was pink and her eyes misty, and to anyone who may have asked—not that there was anyone, damn them all—she would have passed it off as a cold. I figured I knew better.

"Go home, Mama. Go be with Pop," I said, but I knew my words were worthless to the living. A few of the dead looked my way with sympathetic eyes. "Please, go home."

Trinidad remained quietly behind me. He apparently knew that comforting me wasn't necessary. Sad as Mama looked, I actually felt very content. Standing near Mama, I felt the same warm feeling I had with the child on the bridge. I had the desire to offer her comfort, yet receive nothing in return. And if my tattered clothing and bare feet in the dead of winter had not already proven as much, these feelings of pure selflessness convinced me that indeed I was truly dead. Not that I'd been terribly unforgiving or selfish in life, or at least I didn't think I had.

I watched Mama pretend to read a magazine laid out in

front of her because she simply needed something to look at. I glanced at Trinidad, who did not encourage or discourage me as I took a step closer to her. I would have kissed her forehead had I not worried that I'd send her into cardiac arrest at receiving such an invisible touch. Trinidad seemed to know all of these things about me and he smiled.

Then Mama abruptly raised her eyes to stare at me— through me—a me that she could not see. I took a backward step and then another toward her and she repeated the action over again. Incredible. I looked at my companion.

"She knows I'm here?" I was confused and as close to fearful as I could manage. "She is not dying, right?"

Trinidad shook his head. "No. But a mother knows."

I knew that all too well, which immediately brought me to the question that had been tumbling around my disordered brain since my "awakening." Though my peaceful feeling prevented me from becoming truly afraid, I'll admit I was still reluctant to inquire about them.

"Trinidad, where are my children?"

Chapter 4

Barely past the dinner hour, darkness thickly blanketed the small town. As we walked, Christmas lights, still lingering long after the holiday, punctuated the otherwise black neighborhoods, which served as a reminder of my rotten timing, a notion confirmed by my companion. I started to remember things— like seeing the excited expressions on my children's faces as they'd opened their Christmas gifts. Then, I'd managed to die shortly after the holiday, a final morbid gift to my gentle family that would forever link my death to what should be a joyous season.

I assumed Trinidad was taking me to my parents' home, but instead we crossed the street and entered St. Joseph's Cemetery. My footsteps slowed, causing Trinidad to turn to see me. I shook my head.

"No. My children are not here. Please no."

"No." Trinidad dropped back and took my hand. Any panic seemed to dissipate upon his soft touch. "Come."

We weaved between headstones for a while until we came to a clearing that I recognized to be the highest hill directly across the street from my parents' sweet little shake...shingle bungalow. In my bare feet, I stood atop the double plots my folks had purchased years ago for their final resting place. They'd jokingly considered it a premium real estate investment, as they could for all eternity watch over their beloved little house with the white picket fence and flowery backyard.

Near where I stood, frozen black earth had been turned over and had begun to settle, forming a mound that was too new to have a headstone. Trinidad motioned for me to look at the simple marker that had been placed there and despite the darkness my new and improved eyesight allowed me to easily read it.

Laney Cavallo
Beloved Mother, Daughter, Friend

I felt as relieved as the dead can feel that my parents had chosen to put my maiden name on my headstone. My eyes roved over to my parents' large, vacant plots, then to the high chain-link fence that encompassed the cemetery. From there, an embankment steeply rolled down and dropped onto Park Avenue. It was a crystal clear view of my parents' home, sure enough. I was most certain that I was not the guardian they had in mind to eternally mind their residence.

A small black dog burst out of the front door of the house, and seconds later my father appeared in the darkness. He was fast on her heels, pulling on his hat and gloves as he went, muttering all the way, cursing "that damned dog" as he always did. Buttons was old now, but still fairly quick from the looks of it. I'd gotten her from a shelter myself years ago, long before there were lovers and children, careers and cross-country moves.

I watched them for a while then turned toward Trinidad.

"Am I to stay here, to look out for them?"

"No."

I couldn't get impatient, it was impossible, but I made my voice sound as exasperated as I felt it should. "This is all terribly *Our Town*. Will you tell me why I'm here?"

"It's a process. You must understand without a doubt that you are dead. This is where it starts." He looked around and then back at me. "It is important to reconcile where you stand with your god and this earth. You are no longer among the living. You are dead."

I felt close to nervous. I shrugged, half chuckled. "Well, when you say it like that…"

"I'm serious, Laney. You understand it and accept it or we go no further."

I considered it. "Has any dead person ever gone batty on you?"

He didn't laugh.

"There's something wrong, isn't there?" A slow-growing notion of mine was interrupted by another pang of memory. Another flash of blinding light and I squinted my eyes. I heard an engine's roar, smelt the overwhelming odor of fuel and felt us falling. *Us.* I opened my eyes and caught my breath. "Sweet Jesus. My ex, Mark…we were killed in a plane crash."

There were no children in this memory. Still, I needed to be absolutely sure.

"I'd like to see my children please, *now*."

We watched as my father chased that little dog around the yard some more until the mutt finally tired out. He scooped her up, pink tongue hanging out and slushy ice chunks dangling from her perfect Scottie skirt. My father held her against his Carharts, muttering affectionate swears all the way back into the house. He paused at the door and glanced in my direction, and at first I wondered if he sensed I was there as my mother had.

I was struck by the desire to call to him and tell him that I loved him, if mine were the only ears that heard it. I wanted to apologize for every time he would step onto his front porch and his eyes would automatically go to my final resting place. I was truly sorry.

I did none of those things, as I had other things on my

mind, and for the first time I felt I was experiencing genuine postmortem anxiety.

I wanted to see my children immediately.

Chapter 5

"Can I ask you a question?"

My traveling companion looked at me from his first-class seat on an airplane bound for Florida. He arched an eyebrow, surely tired of my questions.

"When we bought our tickets from the…"

He helped me out. "The gentleman at the desk."

I stared at him for a second. "The *dead* guy at the desk. He said it was January."

"January twentieth."

I looked away, my train of thought momentarily disrupted. "Christ, tomorrow is my daughter's birthday. She'll be seven."

Trinidad rubbed his eyes and I noticed he had distinct bands of purple spanning across each fingernail. He was growing frustrated with me. "Do you think you could refrain from using your Lord's name so abusively for even ten minutes?"

"So you are an angel."

"It's not about me being an angel or not being an angel. It's about you using the words Christ and Jesus like some people use the words *and* and *the*. It's excessive and disrespectful to your own fellowship." He quieted when a dead flight attendant shot a nervous glance in our direction. His next words were nearly whispered. "You've got enough issues to reconcile without adding name-calling to the roster."

"What kinds of issues?" Although I was pretty sure I already knew.

"It's not my place to say."

I switched gears. "Trinidad, tell me about your death. Can I call you Trini?"

"No and no," he firmly stated.

"Jesus Christ," I said, though it lacked the smart-aleck tone I'd aimed for. He shot me a look anyway. Being dead hadn't deprived me of my ability to roll my eyes. "Have you ever known any Catholics who *don't* use the Lord's name in vain?"

"It's a needless show of disrespect to religious people."

"Are you a religious person?"

"That's none of your business."

We sighed simultaneously. I slumped in my ridiculously oversized seat. Never in my entire living life had I traveled first class. Figured.

"Then tell me about my death. If it's January and I died on December twenty-seventh, where was I in between then and now?"

Trinidad knew he wasn't going to get any sleep as long as he was with me.

"Dead."

"But I'm dead now." I looked around the largely vacant cabin, whispered, "Was I deader?"

There were minor signs that Trinidad was losing his patience with me. "You were always dead. There's a waiting period."

"Purgatory?"

"Purgatory is a myth. You were resting until your purpose was known."

"That's purgatory."

"No, it's not," he said with mild exasperation. "Trust me though, if there was purgatory you'd only be driving them insane there. You were resting. Period."

I only stared at him until he finally softened. Trinidad's eyes flicked toward the ceiling and then back to mine. "Your value to society was being determined." Then, he rightly assumed that I was about to interrupt him and he touched his fingertips to my lips to shush me. "Sometimes they bring you out. Sometimes if you're good you get to stay in the program."

"Probation?"

He shrugged as if he couldn't explain it himself.

"Well, sounds like purgatory." I picked up a magazine and began to flip through it. A living man exited the bathroom, passed our row and slowed considerably. At first I thought he could see us. Then I realized that he was studying my in-flight reading selection, which I quickly figured to him must have looked like a disembodied magazine floating above the seats. He squinted his eyes shut and was quite startled when a puzzled flight attendant approached him to see if he needed assistance. He promptly ordered a drink and returned to his own seat. Trinidad gave me another one of his disappointed looks and I grinned at him. I could tell this was going to be a standard between us.

"Frankly if they're going to send you to exhume dead folks, they should really equip you with better answers. That's all I'm saying."

"Duly noted."

I looked down at what I was still wearing. "And it wouldn't hurt to bring a little change of wardrobe, either. I'm seeing all these dead people in rags."

"They're fine for now." He adjusted his seat to recline a little and closed his eyes.

"And one more thing."

"With you, I doubt it."

"Isn't it a little insensitive to put me on a plane after I just crashed and burned in one a little less than a month ago?"

"It's not like you risk dying if we do crash." He fluffed his marshmallow-sized pillow. "I'm going to rest now, thank you."

I blinked as I considered it. "Wait—do we *need* sleep?"

"No. But I enjoy the meditation."

"Well, I don't need to meditate or rest," I muttered in a tone more sarcastic than I probably should be using with an angel or otherwise spiritual tour guide. "I've been resting for nearly a month. What do I need with rest now?"

But soon enough I closed my eyes, not out of tiredness, but out of boredom. With all risk virtually erased and with a totally nonproductive existence—or nonexistence, as the case may be—I was amazed at how utterly bored I felt. Knowing I could look forward to seeing my children once again and very soon, I turned my thoughts toward them.

The slight, constant tremble of the plane lulled me into a strange, meditative state. After a bit I saw another flash, and again could smell leaking fuel. In my mind's eye, I watched as we endlessly plummeted to the earth. Sparks flew, then impact. I startled slightly and my eyelids sprang open. Trinidad was awake and watching me.

There were no fearful feelings attached to these flashbacks, only the surprise of recalling even more details of the last event of my life; the event that had resulted in me now being on a plane headed for Florida with a dead man seated next to me.

Chapter 6

"We're here."

Trinidad nudged me alert and I literally sprang to my feet. Before, I'd have felt my back popping, knees creaking, and feet tingling after such a long flight. Those general aches and pains I'd spent thirty-nine years accumulating—and alternatively ignoring—were now only a memory. I felt...good.

I listened to the flight announcement and turned to Trinidad.

"Is Orlando our destination or do we have a connecting flight?"

Even the bright cabin lights flickering to life didn't bother my eyes, and I found I could now read from incredible distances, too. I zeroed in on a list no bigger than five inches square with about a twelve point font, posted above a cabinet in the flight attendant's area. It was an outdated cheat sheet for dealing with difficult passengers and how to identify and alert an air marshal.

It was crystal clear—I'd never need to squint again. Being dead was incredible. And weird.

"Indeed it is." That was Trinidad being vague again.

"We live in New York. Me and the kids and Mara—" I stopped abruptly, felt Trinidad staring at me with an air of self-righteousness. I quietly amended my statement. "My family lived in New York."

"Your children live in a suburb of this city. I'm taking you there now."

I knew better than to ask about it again. Even dead, I felt some frustration with Trinidad's poor communication skills. Alive, I might have been livid about it.

We basically hitchhiked to our destination, silently tagging along with the living on two different cab rides. Another Dead accompanied us on our first ride. He nodded hello to us, then rested his stovepipe hat on his lap as he took a seat up front next to the oblivious driver. As I had been many times in real life, I was stuck straddling the bump in the middle of the backseat, wedged between Trinidad and a living paying passenger. I amused myself by waving my hand slowly before his eyes and leaning my face terribly close to his. Nothing.

Bored, I turned my attention outside the cab and saw many Deads. I was getting very good at spotting them by now. For the most part, their clothing gave them away. That and the strange habit Deads had for engaging in activities one would not normally perform at nearly six o'clock in the morning. Like whooping it up at outdoor barbeques with other Deads, or selling flowers curbside. Seeing the child-Deads playing together made me as close to uncomfortable as I could be in my condition, though oddly they seemed happiest of all. And all the Deads, young and old, seemed to realize that we were traveling past. Often a Dead would look up from gardening or bike riding, or even abandon an antique push cart of flowers to give us a little wave. As surreal as it all was, one thing puzzled me more than anything else.

"What's with the animals?" I whispered. A dog in the cab's passenger seat flicked it's ears back and turned around to see me. I gulped and smiled and wondered if it knew what I was saying.

"There's no need to whisper. The living cannot hear you."

So I loudly said, "The dog is staring at me."

"Animals are inherently pure and good. Their senses are ultra keen. Small children can see you, too, so mind your behavior." Trinidad motioned toward the living driver, who'd begun to talk to the dog as he scrubbed his pet affectionately behind the ears. "That dog can see you as if you were just as alive as his owner there."

So animals could see the dead, which gave me a whole new wonderment about what invisible things they were really sniffing at as they dragged their owners around town by their leashes. I began to wonder how many Deads had existed among us in the West Village with its history-rich buildings. I wondered how many of them had hurriedly stepped out of the way to avoid being stepped on by me, and much of the time I found myself believing this was all one big, bizarre dream. I hoped not because I desperately wanted to see my children.

Our journey ended in a place called Pine Crest, a gated, swank country club community with new Southern-style mansions and perfectly manicured lawns. I wondered how my children had come to live in such a place.

I thought about our tiny two-bedroom apartment in New York, its carefully crafted nooks and crannies bulging with children's stuffed animals and books, soap dishes overflowing with too many bath toys, and closets that risked springing forth and raining down a storm of clothes, coats, shoes, seasonal decorations, vacuum cleaners—whatever was necessary to keep us from going insane inside nine hundred square feet. I thought about cleverly built bunks in a childlike room that were barely slept in, and about a queen-sized bed in the next room that generally had four pairs of feet dangling from the end of it. It was cozy and sweet, a world away from these pretentious surroundings.

We pulled very near the driveway of one such tricked-out home, three stories high with white pillars that went all the way to the top. I estimated it to be no smaller than ten thousand square feet, with a sprawling lawn twice that size. While the living passenger negotiated his payment with the cabbie,

Trinidad and I easily slipped through the cab window and headed toward a circular stone driveway wrapped around an immense artsy water fountain.

"Who lives here?" I asked, not hiding my astonishment. I wondered if dead tour guides were ever wrong. Now, anything seemed possible.

"Your children do."

"With who?"

"With whom," he politely corrected me.

We followed the driveway to a connecting brick path that led to a side door. The sign posted read "Service Entrance" and there was a doorbell. I waited to see if Trinidad would press it and if a Dead would answer. Instead, he simply turned the knob and let us in.

"You've been here before?" I followed him to a steep staircase that wound up the rear quarters of the impersonal extravagance someone was calling home.

"No," he answered.

We reached the second floor of the near-royal home and I followed Trinidad down a wide hallway. He nudged open one of the doors leading to the pinkest, frilliest bedroom I'd ever seen. My daughter lay sleeping on a bed fit for a princess. Her younger brother was curled at her feet, tangled in a small blanket. I wanted to run to them, scoop them up and hug them tight. At the same time, if my appearance frightened them, it would surely break my heart, dead or not.

It felt like it took me forever to reach my children, and I perched myself on the edge of the bed near my son. It took everything I had to resist running my fingers through Cooper's curly golden-brown hair. I gently pulled the blankets around his tiny shoulders. Another curly head, only with longer hair, was asleep on the pillow. My precious Bella. Suddenly, I felt every bit of that full month I'd been away from them during my "deader" time. I wanted my children more than anything.

I looked at Trinidad, whispered, "Please explain."

He misunderstood my question. "Your boy is afraid of the dark. He sneaks in here at night to sleep."

"They are both afraid of the dark," I explained to him.

My gaze flitted around the room, noting the closed door and the floor-to-ceiling windows that were shut up tight. Though I could see perfectly well, I knew it must be horrifyingly dark to a small child. I heard myself rambling. "They don't like it dark and they don't like the bedroom door closed. They need the window cracked and city sounds to sleep. How can they possibly sleep here at all?"

"Children adapt."

"But who do they live with in such a place?" And as I was considering exploring the pristine quarters, I heard a woman's heavily accented southern voice on the other side of the bedroom door. I looked at Trinidad. My eyes were wide. "We have to go! The children can't see me like this!"

Chapter 7

I did not want to scare Bella and Cooper with my raggedy, singed appearance. That aside, I was also *dead*.

Trinidad and I made a mad dash for a huge walk-in closet that was as stylish and as chock-full of clothes as a designer boutique. Well hidden for the time being, I peered through a sliver of an opening and watched my children slowly rouse from sleep.

A rotund African-American woman waddled into the room, trilling good morning greetings all the way. She was dressed in maid attire reminiscent of something worn in the Civil War era, complete with white pantyhose and matching orthopedic-looking shoes that made a little squish-squish sound when she waddled. She wore a fluffy bonnet over her hair. Her dress and throwback accent had me puzzled as to her...*condition*.

"Living," Trinidad clarified, as if he'd read my mind.

We watched her toddle and sway her way over to the bed.

"Good morning, children! Out of bed with you. Up! Up!" She tousled my son's hair as I had longed to do. Her smile was broad and genuine, which caused me to warm to her a little. "Little man, you shouldn't be asleep in your sister's bed. You know the trouble you'd be in. You've got to be a big boy."

Talking all the while in her southern melodic voice, the maid assisted Cooper in getting down from the high bed. She made me uncomfortable with her gentle, albeit Jemima tone and attitude, evidence of an ancient southern blackness so marked, I could feel her repression from the afterlife. But Trinidad seemed quite positive that indeed she was a Living. She went on. "You know what the missus says about that nonsense, don't you?"

"Are you going to tell her?" Cooper asked in his sweet, childish lisp.

The maid shook her head and moved toward the head of the bed, fluffing pillows all the way. "No sir, I won't." She nudged my daughter next. "Darlin'? Time to get up. Come now. Nanny didn't come in today. *Again*. So, I've got to get you down to breakfast."

The small bed lump twisted in place and issued a weak verbal protest. But it was the maid who had my undivided attention at that moment. She had turned around and was headed straight for our closet shelter.

It was a spacious walk-in, at least as large as our entire bedroom in New York, so getting out of her way was not the problem. If Trinidad was right and children could see Deads, avoiding having Bella and Cooper see us standing there in the openness of the highly organized closet—*that* was the problem. I saw a door on the opposite wall and made a run for it. Trinidad followed me and we'd barely had a chance to make our escape when the maid yanked the double doors wide open.

The adjoining room was a bathroom with two sinks, a tub the size of a small pool, a shower that rivaled anything I'd ever seen in a spa advertisement, and a bidet and a toilet. But my eyes were already focused on still another door. I quickly opened it.

My son's new room was also oversized and every bit as blue as Bella's was pink. It was too feminine and devoid of any of his favorite things. No GI Joes, no dozens of matchbox cars scattered everywhere, and, I sadly noted, no tattered security blanket lying in a heap on the floor. It was impeccable with lush comforters and woven floor coverings, the only obvious toy being a rather juvenile-looking wooden rocking horse and mobile of blue clowns dangling over a bed as huge and high as my daughter's new one. My son hates clowns.

I tiptoed across to the other door (as if tiptoeing would matter) and stepped into the hallway. The maid was fast, already there and issuing last-minute orders about brushing teeth and wearing matching socks. I stayed perfectly still against the wall where she would not bump into me. Trinidad was across the wide hallway, already headed toward another door. He paused and waited for me to join him. I prayed that I knew exactly who would be on the other side of that door; prayed that Mara had miraculously inherited a ton of money from some long-lost family member, thereby affording her such a home. Perhaps she'd had the place professionally decorated in advance of their arrival, which could explain the uncharacteristic and pretentious children's rooms. I admit it was a faint hope, at best.

Trinidad gave the door a gentle push and opened it to reveal a petite woman hustling across the bedroom, pinning blond hair into a perfect upsweep.

Disappointment washed through me as I watched the unfamiliar female backside adjust the collar of a rather lavish dress before slipping into a pair of Manolos so high they would surely have thrown my back out of alignment in my living years. Only when she looked in the mirror did I finally get a glimpse of her face. I moved in for a closer look as she tucked a few errant hairs behind her ear. When she turned around my heart nearly stopped. It was my old best friend, Tatum Conway.

Tate, as I'd called her in college, swore she was born to be a southern belle, and *Gone with the Wind* was her favorite movie—all things that were rapidly explaining the maid and the ridiculously flowery home. In reality, she was from the backwoods of Missouri, somewhere in the middle of twelve children, a drunken goat farmer for a father who housed them in a shack that didn't even have plumbing, and that is a true story. She was smart, though her purpose at the University of South Carolina (the school where we'd met years ago; the school I subsequently dropped out of) was not to study statistics and math, which she was naturally good at; rather, it was to land a fine southern gentleman. Having already pulled herself out of the gutter to achieve a top-notch education, she'd been convinced she could do anything, which was probably right. Tate swore she'd live on a plantation one day. It appeared that they'd started building faux plantations on the fringes of golf courses in Florida.

I took another look around the amazing home with its artistic, hand-bordered ceilings higher than I'd seen in museums. I mouthed "wow" to no one. I supposed this house could be the modern—age version of her fifteen-year-old dream. I supposed she'd found her Rhett.

In our younger years, Tate and I had taken annual beach vacations until just after Bella was born. Afterward, I'd invited her to visit countless times, but she'd flatly refused, claiming to have "an extreme adverse reaction" to Mark. Most people did. He'd detested our girl-getaways, called Tate catty and a few other choice things. Thanks to my crystal clear memory, I now remembered those events in better detail than I wanted to.

I'd once entered Tate's name in the pool for godmother for my daughter, more for the reaction that I knew it would draw from Mark. He did not disappoint, never missing an opportunity to fly into a good fury, and he tore my list into pieces. I could not imagine that any such document existed these days that would indicate Tate be named godmother. After helping to raise at least half her siblings, she previously claimed to have no leftover desire to parent. However, this could explain the babyish, overdone rooms; she probably didn't even know what was age appropriate, and certainly she wouldn't know what their preferences were. It did not explain why the children were not residing with the guardian I'd very *specifically* named for them as recently as four years ago.

I watched Tate apply and blot lipstick and curl long eyelashes. She tied a Chanel scarf around her neck and fluffed out the ends. The end result was over the top, but probably fantastic by male standards. I thought she looked a little like a flight attendant.

"My God, is Mara okay?"

"Shh."

"Is Tate a good guardian at least?" I asked Trinidad. He only shushed me again.

Tate snatched a tiny bag off the bed and I started to duck out of her way, but Trinidad grabbed my arm to stop me from leaving. He stared straight into my eyes and no joy shone there. I knew I was about to learn something of importance that I would probably not enjoy. A voice drew me out of my head and I turned around. Were it not for the impossibility of the dead passing out cold, I surely would have.

Fresh from the shower, wearing a short towel and the grin of an extremely happy man, was my husband. And I assure you he was very much alive.

Chapter 8

Mark Anderson stepped toward Tatum and wrapped his arms around her. He squeezed her until she giggled like a school girl. She threw her head back, giving him opportunity to kiss her neck.

"You're getting me all wet," she hissed in the most ridiculous fake southern drawl I'd ever heard, alive or dead.

"Well then, mission accomplished," he teased.

His towel "accidentally" slipped away and fell to the floor, revealing his trim, toned physique. He made a low growl.

Apparently the dead cannot become nauseated.

"Stop it, Marcus!" Tatum playfully swatted at him. "You'll make me late for the Pine Crest Ladies Breakfast."

Marcus? Not even at birth.

"Pine Crest doesn't have ladies. None that I've met anyways."

Mark-the-heathen made no effort at faking a Southern

accent, which actually would have been preferable to his normal tone. He was born and bred (possibly inbred) in Arkansas, but I'd never known other Arkansas folks to possess such an extreme grating hick-accent. I could appreciate the annoyance even in my condition.

The pair advanced their repulsive play all the way to the preposterous Scarlett O'Hara bed, and that's when I started for the door. Though there was no danger that my husband would hear me because he was alive, I waited until Trinidad and I were well in the hallway before I let it fly.

"Tell me anything you think I might possibly want to know—starting with how that philandering fuck is still alive." I was a little surprised that I could say "fuck" in my postmortem tongue, and even more surprised that Trinidad had wisely chosen not to reprimand me for my choice of language. "Go on. I'm all ears."

He nodded. "What do you remember about the crash?"

We stared at each other for several seconds. I sighed, and with some reluctance closed my eyes.

"Smell of fuel. Black smoke, sparks…" I impatiently narrated my increasingly emergent recollection. "The plane fell out of the sky. Bam—I'm dead." I opened my eyes, looked at Trinidad blankly. "That's everything I remember."

He reached out, rested his hand on my arm. "Try again."

I closed my eyes for several seconds. The vision was clearer this time, as if someone had adjusted the antennae on an old TV. In this new hi-def, I heard and felt things with such remarkable clarity, when at last I opened my eyes I was as mad as a Dead could get. "That son of a bitch ejected himself from the plane."

Trinidad removed his hand from me, and leaned back on his heels, patiently awaiting any other revelations I might have. I did have other thoughts and I sorted through, discarded the practical ones and embraced any emotion I could within my newly blunted emotional confines.

"He hates Tate!"

"Does he?"

"He cursed her very existence!" I practically spat. "How did this happen?"

Trinidad issued what I perceived to be a smug little smile. He lowered his chin almost to his chest and spoke in a confessional tone. "Sometimes people have entirely secret lives, don't you agree? Secret longings?"

I ignored his insinuation. "So what's the point of bringing me here—for me to witness the lonely widower having a roll in the hay with the southern trollop?" I laughed, muttered, "Not interested. Thanks."

"I guess you wouldn't be."

I'd had it. "Exactly what do you want to say to me, Trinidad? Because you've been beating around the bush about stuff ever since we met up, which, frankly, is something only a real pansy-ass angel would do. If you've got some sort of judgment to pass on me, do it and damn well get it over with!"

"It's not my place to pass judgment."

"And yet you manage to uphold such an outstanding level of self-righteousness." I lowered my gaze to match his. "My mistake for thinking an angel of God would have some integrity."

"For the last time, I am not an angel." His words were calm and he emanated only serenity.

Not me. For having no ability to get truly angry, I was doing a pretty good job of getting worked up.

"Did *Marcus* want me dead?" I emphasized his phony name. "Do you mean to tell me that he wasn't just a dumb-ass of a pilot? He took me away from my children just so he could have Tate? We were fine on our own! I stuck to the agreement— divorce after five years—that's what he said!"

"Calm down."

"Oh…I should have known better than to get on that toy-sized plane with him. Tricked again! I should have known he'd never stick to his word—the weasel!"

"Laney, calm down."

"He's alive and I'm dead," I said, pointing toward the bedroom where the merry widower was getting his freak on with Miss Scarlett. My voice had returned to its new quiet, but there was no mistaking my anger. "Let's review—alive. *Dead.* And this is my hell. How'm I doing so far?"

Contrary to the annoyance he'd displayed during our plane

ride, Trinidad regarded me with exceeding patience.

He seemed to project his calmness onto me. It washed through my body, causing my shoulders to slump and my thoughts to shift dramatically. I stared at the horrid faux red Persian carpet, even traced part of the pattern with my bare toe.

I mentally reviewed the upside: the children were healthy and being cared for. My children have always been my priority. Once I was satisfied that they were at least safe, a different question emerged as the new frontrunner. Trinidad knew my query before I could ask it, for he realized that in life I'd been very much in love.

In life it truly never occurred to me that those religious fanatics had been right in their condemnation of gays. I looked straight into Trinidad's eyes hoping to find the truth and suddenly afraid of it at the same time. I asked the burning question. "Tell me, Trinidad, am I being punished because the love of my life was a woman?"

He didn't answer right away.

I quietly said, "I would like to see Mara. Please."

After several long seconds, he reached out and clasped my hand. "Close your eyes."

Chapter 9

Our apartment was an old converted four-story horse stable in the West Village on Eighth Street, mere blocks from the Hudson. Standing on the rooftop, with the Statue of Liberty at your back in the distance, one could see every major building made famous on a New York postcard.

The street below was a social hub. There was a private school for grades pre-K through eight across the street that I was particularly fond of because my children went there. Shipping docks were no more than a quarter of a mile away. Water taxis hauling tourists made regular stops at the nearby Pier 45. Despite being plunked right in the midst of this noisy center, our home was deathly quiet on this day.

My companion's dream-like tour followed along a stretch of narrow hallway until it dead-ended into two bedroom doors. The door to the left was shut, which was unusual in itself. The stillness of the tiny closed-off quarters could be felt all the way from where I now stood, and I did not ask to look inside. I knew I would see my children's things scattered everywhere in a place where children no longer lived, and I could not bear to witness that.

The only other bedroom had a set of glass French doors and I nodded for Trinidad to advance our view inside because I knew who I would find there.

My sweet Mara lay stretched out across the bed we'd shared for five years. She wore jeans and a wrinkled sweater that looked like it was left over from at least the day before. Her normally radiant complexion was pale, and dark half circles underscored her puffy eyes. In her sleep she did not look like her usual tower of strength. She looked spent, tired, tinier than ever and downright old, bless her. Knowing my Mara, I could safely assume it was her first true sleep in days. I wondered how long it had been since she'd shown her face at the university. They surely missed her. My Mara is brilliant.

I longed to reach out and stroke the hair away from her eyes and speak sweetly to her, much as she had done to me whenever I was in need. But my vision of her was merely on loan from my companion. I opened my eyes because I was ready to leave it. Indeed Trinidad had honored my request, but I felt no better for knowing the truth.

He unclasped my hand, but I continued to stare at him hoping he would supply me with answers without my begging them from him. He only patiently waited.

"This is what I did to the people around me," I whispered at last, my shoulders slightly caving inward. "This is the hell I've created for all of us because I was stupid enough to get into a ridiculously tiny airplane with my jerk of an ex-husband."

Trinidad's interruption surprised me. "He wasn't your ex."

"Close enough. Now my children have been uprooted from their lives and are being raised by strangers. And Mara is...*suffering*." I felt vacant, unable to access proper emotions or words. I looked into his eyes. "Are these the repercussions for me being gay? For loving a woman? Jesus—don't tell me those crazy religious zealots were right."

"No." Trinidad spoke with conviction. "The Creator knows the true heart."

"I loved her with all my heart, Trinidad. That simply cannot be wrong." I shook my head sadly. "God knows that, right?"

He looked at me for a moment and sighed. "You should have gotten a proper divorce, Laney."

His alleging that I'd led a two-timing lifestyle sounded as absurd as everything else I'd learned in the past twelve hours. "You think I'm an adulterer? God is angry despite everything I endured? I was protecting my family!"

"You're no dummy—you know what you should have done. The Creator doesn't appreciate arrogance of those who think they can bypass the system," he said, softly flicking the collar of my shredded, burnt lambskin jacket. He whispered, "And frankly, your Saint Francis isn't crazy about that coat, either."

My eyes widened at his strange near-accusation, but the sound of my children returning from their breakfast rapidly changed the subject. They exploded out of the stairway landing and attacked me with the force of a tyke-sized army. It did not seem to faze them that I was wearing torn and tattered clothing or a dead animal coat. After several rounds of hugging and kissing, I ushered Cooper and Bella into the frilly pink room to avoid having anyone downstairs hear their gleeful, childish screams.

"Where have you been, Mommy?" Cooper climbed me like a jungle gym and it felt good to have my little boy back in my arms. "We missed you!"

Bella's words went straight to my core. "Are you going to take us home now?"

I looked for Trinidad, but he had quietly left me to my children. I was in charge of my own words, and I wanted to choose careful answers for my children to avoid confusing or hurting them any more than they already had been. In life, I'd been the residential motivational speaker for my children and my lover. As a Dead, I wasn't sure how those skills would stack up.

I sat down on the edge of the oversized bed and gathered my children onto my lap. I tried to find a good place to start and there did not seem to be one, but I started anyway.

"I was in a plane accident. With Mark."

"He said we should call him daddy." Cooper wrinkled his lightly freckled button nose. "I don't want to call him that."

"Oh, this is tough," I said more to me than to them. "Mark is your biological father, baby. That means that he gave you to me like a little gift. When you were born, Mama Mara and I took care of you and we both love you and your sister very much. We've always felt very lucky and thankful to Mark for helping us have you."

It was a softened-up, abridged version of the truth, a reality I'd painted on the spot because it was prettier than anything else I could say about Mark and his parenting skills or lack thereof. Mara and I knew there would come a day when a full explanation would be required for this child, but I didn't plan on it being today, in my present condition, and without Mara beside me. It's true I was the motivator, but Mara was definitely the voice of reason in our world.

"I remembered Mark," Bella said, looking more solemn than I'd ever seen her. She accusingly repeated, "I remembered him, all right."

She didn't say anything else; she didn't have to. I nodded and sadly smiled at her. I was still looking for outstanding pieces to the puzzle that had become my nonexistence. "What did Mark tell you had happened to Mommy?"

Cooper's eyes flitted thoughtfully toward the ceiling and then back to me. "He said that you died in an accident." He stumbled over the big word. "He said that you were not coming back because you moved to heaven. Did you move there, Mommy? Are you an angel now?"

It was laughable that Mark would speak of anything remotely biblical. I was surprised he'd even take that creative license for the children's sake. I wondered if he cared for my kids in any way whatsoever. Given the apparent situation, I hoped to Christ he did.

I didn't want to lie to them, and clearly I didn't know where I stood in the "system." I blinked hard and when I reopened my eyes, Trinidad was standing behind my children, out of their view. He nodded his approval for the story I was about to weave.

"Yes," I whispered. "I am an angel."

"Where are your wings then?" Puzzled, Cooper looked at my back.

I thought of Clarence in *It's a Wonderful Life* and I smiled. "I'm earning them."

Trinidad arched an eyebrow in a comedic fashion and I stifled my laughter. I suppose they'd had no cable television in Bangladesh.

"Mommy, did it hurt to die?"

Bella's concern nearly melted me. I hugged her close, profoundly glad that I was only devoid of my sense of taste and not touch. I needed them as physically close to me as possible.

"No, sweetie, it didn't." I smiled at her, pressed a dozen tiny kisses on her forehead. And though I had no recollection of my final moments beyond seeing my pilot eject himself, I elaborated anyway. "I went to sleep thinking about you and Cooper and how much I loved you both. And I will always love you very, very much."

They seemed satisfied with my death summarization in which I'd made the whole process sound almost appealing. I didn't even look in Trinidad's direction.

"I don't like Mark. He says he's going to make me into a real man. I already am a big man, right Mommy?" Cooper said, his tiny brow furrowing again.

I can't say I didn't see that one coming. I could only imagine how surprised and angry Mark must have been to discover that he had a curly-haired, sweet-faced son he wasn't aware of— being raised by a couple of lesbians—oh boy. Knowing what a fool-headed manly-man Mark was, I was a little surprised he'd allowed Scarlet to decorate the boy's room with such an effeminate flourish. I figured he'd have the place outfitted in camouflage and all things militia to try and undo the effects of lesbian childrearing on his only son.

"You are my big man," I calmly assured him.

"And there's no gold chair here," Cooper babbled on. He was referring to the chair in our apartment designated as a "calm down" chair when my son got wheezy or displayed other prerequisites of an asthma attack. "And I didn't get to bring my little men, and there's no markers and no…" He rambled on his gentle way, condemning everything in his new life, from Mark's hot temper to having been forced to try cold soup he called gauze poncho. I tried to listen to him, nodded all the while, but my concentration was focused solely on holding him tight.

"Mark is trying to get to know you, that's all, sweetie. Give him some time, could you?"

"You want me to be extra-extra patient with him?"

I'd often asked him to be "extra-extra patient" with a particularly immature neighbor boy in our building. Hearing Cooper issue my own words back to me made me grin hard.

"Yes, that would be really nice of you."

"How did you know we would be here?" Bella chimed in at last. "How did you get here? When do you have to go back?"

"A friend brought me here."

"Another angel?"

I nodded again. And though I wasn't exactly sure what mission was to be accomplished by Trinidad bringing me to Florida, I was glad to see my girl on her special day. "I wanted to wish you Happy Birthday, sweetie. I'll stay as long as I possibly can. Okay?"

They nodded.

"And I think it might be a good idea if we kept my visit a little secret." I tried to gauge their reactions. "That'd be kinda fun, right?"

"Do you hurt now?" Bella again. I shook my head. "Do you promise?" She looked contemplative as she took a mini-inventory of my scorched clothing.

"Bella, honey, I promise I feel very, very good."

"Okay," she said before diving in with the question that pinged me hard, even in the afterlife. "When can we go home to Mama Mara?"

Chapter 10

Bella's birthday party was a literally a headliner. At least a hundred well-to-do folks had emerged from their valet-parked Mercedes and Beamers to comprise a mix that looked like the Who's Who of the Fortune 500. A colorful, brilliantly lit canopy at least the size of the house was pitched on the back lawn with heaters lining the perimeter, blasting warm air onto the revelers. The hosts had thought of everything. Bella's birthday party could have easily been mistaken for a wedding had it not been for the three-ring circus of acrobats, clowns, and a small petting zoo of animals creating a virtually palatial extravaganza.

Considering that it was a child's birthday, the kids appeared to be an afterthought. A league of nannies and other hired entertainers shepherded them around, keeping them out of harm's way and more importantly, I suspected, out of their parents' hair. At the moment they were huddled around a baby elephant, and I wondered how much the Florida humidity, coupled with this exposure to animals, was aggravating my son's asthma.

Men in white pants and women in lopping hats laughed and threw back cocktails. It was terribly Hampton-esque. Trinidad and I roamed through the party leisurely and, naturally, unnoticed.

"I'll bet there's a high ratio of women named Cricket to men with Roman numerals after their name."

"Be nice."

"I'm plenty nice, Trini. But you have to admit that the concentration of ostentatious douche bags on this lawn is so dense you can feel it from the afterlife." He shot me an advisory look, but I wasn't sure if it was for me calling him Trini or for my creative terminology. I wasn't worried about it, really; he'd already pegged me for an adulterer, after all. What harm was adding foul-mouthed to that label?

"And who hires a photographer to take birthday pictures? Bust out the Canon Sure-Shot already."

Trinidad's eyes followed the gentleman toting a magnificent lens around, snapping random shots of the crowd. "That's a newspaper photographer. He's covering the event."

I mouthed the word "event" and watched the hobnobbers with disgust.

"Don't be judgmental. It's not the example you want to set for your children," Trinidad said, and he was off, snaking through the crowd, dodging randomly placed oversized chocolate fountains and sporadic bistro tables. I was hot on his heels.

Ahead of us, a waiter had half a dozen drinks teetering on his tray in a precarious equilibrium. With lightning speed, Trinidad snatched away a particularly wobbly champagne flute, saving it from triggering certain disaster. The waiter didn't even notice as he continued on his route. Trinidad held the saved glass somewhat awkwardly. I grabbed it away from him with the same quick motion he'd used with the waiter. I tossed it back with great theatrics and chugged it down smoothly, something I wouldn't have been able to achieve in my living years. There was no taste and no effect. I had a feeling if I'd had a beer bong,

I'd have been a hit at an afterlife frat house. I wiped my lips on my singed sleeve and bowed, somewhat pleased that I was disgusting him.

"Want me to get you another?" I sweetly offered.

He shook his head. "My religion does not permit me to imbibe."

I thought back to my first glass of wine, age six, after Mass. "Really? My religion promotes it."

"I don't drink," he reaffirmed more solidly.

"Trini, you're dead," I reminded him.

I nearly bumped into a bored woman trapped in a lengthy one-sided conversation with a real stiff—a suited up, hunch-shouldered fellow with Roosevelt glasses who was rambling in a monotone that I'm sure had her wanting to trade places with me. Well, maybe not. I snatched a drink off another passing tray and wedged the glass stem between her fingers. She looked surprised, yet didn't seem to care where it had come from. I giggled like a schoolgirl as she drank it down with almost as much aplomb as I'd downed mine. She looked grateful, and much happier. Trinidad tsked at me.

I shrugged, wide-eyed. "What? I just answered her prayer."

"Let us go," he insisted.

I glanced in the distraught bimbo's direction. "She'll need another drink, trust me." But he didn't wait for me. I sighed loudly. Clearly my miracle-making was not appreciated by my companion. "Fine, I'm coming."

We slipped through the back door and wove through the hustle and bustle that was taking place in the commercial-grade kitchen. I would have previously taken the smell of seafood to be a mouthwatering nirvana, but this time a stack of lobsters with their claws tightly bound looked at me with fearful beady eyes that spoke of their impending doom. They were making sounds I'd never heard out of lobsters before. A particular one, I swear, was trying to speak to me, his tinny, pleading voice wavering pathetically, begging for rescue, which freaked me out so much I almost crashed into a server with a tray full of picnic-style salads. Trinidad grabbed my arm and steered me away from potential chaos and out of the room. From behind us I heard the scream of the poor, ill-fated creature, a sound that was so dreadful and pleading, I clenched my eyes shut and covered my ears.

When I opened my eyes again, Trinidad's hands were clamped on my shoulders, shaking me alert. We were in the hallway outside wide pane-glass doors that led to a lavish study. We walked in without interrupting a different kind of party that had no kids, but definitely clowns, sucking lines of coke through straws made of hundred dollar bills. My husband was one of the idiots, his lovely plaything curled up on his lap, sitting amidst half a dozen other high society fools. Their noses were powdered up and they sat there, sniffing, laughing, and making small talk. When the conversation grew stilted, it was obvious the three men wanted to speak without the presence of the women. The campaign for their absence was spearheaded by Mark in his uncouth tongue.

"Why don't you go check on the children, Tatie?"

Except for Tatum, the women in attendance seized their cue, stood, brushed off their skirts or slacks and scrubbed their knuckles under their nostrils to eliminate any telltale residue of their afternoon tryst.

"Thank you, darling, but I'll stay," Tatum replied through her tight smile.

Not one to take shit from his woman—I could certainly attest to that—Mark raised his voice a little, his lips slightly twitching as he made the suggestion a second time.

"It's Bella's birthday. She'll want her mother to watch her open her presents."

I bristled at hearing him refer to Tatum as "Bella's mother."

"I don't think another fifteen minutes will make or break my mother-of-the-year award, do you, darling?" Her tone was flat and her glare matched his.

They engaged each other in a silent standoff, neither one succumbing to so much as an eye twitch. I had to admit that Mark may have truly met his match in this one.

"All right," he said, deflated, visibly displeased at having been put in his place in front of his colleagues. Tatum stayed put while the other modelesque wives made their exit, apparently not ready—if ever—to take their own husbands to task in front of a group of any size.

Tatum slid her pristine bottom into the expensive leather chair next to Mark. She started the proceedings. Big surprise.

Her voice was a husky southern drawl as she addressed the man seated across from her. "Tim, I trust you're working through those EPA issues with the numbers, am I right?"

I recognized Tim Nelson, an attorney for the Environmental Protection Agency, from having butted heads with him from both an environmental perspective and a personal one—he was also Mark's longtime private counsel. I recalled his involvement in my unsuccessful campaign to get a divorce, but that's another story. I quickly figured out which role he was representing this afternoon.

I remember Mark first introducing Nelson to me as being his oldest—and I daresay perhaps his only—friend. Nelson looked considerably older and his stress-pinched face was orange-tanned. I wondered if he'd also transplanted himself to the Sunshine State or had hit a fake-and-bake booth before heading south to better fit in. If the latter was the case, he scored a big old fail.

"It's been…trying, but we're finally moving forward."

"What's the timeline on that?"

Nelson looked put on the spot. "Well, I can't be sure. But we're still waiting for patents and clearance from the USDA, so what's the hurry?"

I whispered to Trinidad regardless of the fact that they could not hear me, "What are they talking about?"

Trinidad only shushed me, his eyes never leaving the small crew seated in the study.

"Two *USDA* friends have a vested monetary interest in the product." She leaned over and sexily swept her fingertips through Mark's hair. "We don't foresee any problems getting it passed through the system fairly quickly."

Nelson seemed shocked. He lowered his brandy glass, arched an eyebrow. "That's illegal as hell."

"No more illegal than having an EPA fellow onboard." She struck a thoughtful pose, smiled sweetly, asked, "Do we have one of those, Tim?"

Nelson regarded her with sheer mistrust. She couldn't be making his life easy.

I nudged Trinidad. "What does *Tatie* do for a living?"

"She's recently retired from an investment brokerage."

I looked around at the lush carpets and rich mahogany bookcases that lined the room. The mansion had to be hers. I'd left Mark living in a wonderful, but much less exotic ranch-style home in Newark, New Jersey, and try as I might, I couldn't seem to connect any dots that would have him ending up here. "What were they brokering? Humans? Drugs? How can she afford all this?"

Clearly I wasn't picking the information out of the conversation that Trinidad intended I should. He rolled his eyes, nudged me toward the door. Soon enough we were back outside, cruising right through the elaborate big top. I caught a glimpse of Bella's forlorn expression as she sat in the center of a circle of children she'd probably known for all of an hour. I felt proud as I watched her there with her arm draped protectively over her little brother. They were surrounded by strangers, effectively keeping their distance from them.

I thought about Bo Peep and her flock in the library and their afternoon snack and wondered if they were dealing drugs. But all the talk of patents and government agencies had my brain pointed in a different direction; a road that I'd nearly traveled once before. My feet seemed to move in slow motion as we bypassed the party crowd, headed for a building no larger than a potting shed. I paid particular attention to my feet as I walked lightly on the springy grass, nearly floating as we made our way, and it had nothing at all to do with being dead or even heavenly, as I'd hinted to my children. A vague notion that tickled my brain solidified itself once we'd entered the shed.

I stood in the center of the building and slowly turned full circle, mouth agape, eyes wide.

Chapter 11

Seventeen years before I, uh…died, I was screwing off my third year of college. I made guest appearances in all my classes, and then only if I wasn't tired from having stayed up writing all night long. I'd write anything—poetry, short stories, books fat enough to rival a Stephen King novel—by quantity only, not quality. I held a brief position with the campus newspaper and later I held down the fort at the college yearbook when the advisory professor had a nervous breakdown. I was eventually fired from both jobs for trying to make them less politically stagnant.

I never considered myself radical by any stretch of the imagination, but I confess that I was also kicked out of a journalism class thanks to my tendency to ride freedom of the press full speed to its very fringe. In fact, if I ran into James Madison in the afterlife, I figured I'd better duck him or risk getting bitch-slapped.

For similar reasons I was also subsequently discharged from my creative writing class. For being a relatively quiet girl, my acidy, liberal pen had much to say. Mostly, I spent my time penning back—porch poetry and drinking with the other socially rebellious angst-ridden campus drinkers, not to a deleterious degree, but enough to realize that I wasn't achieving anything in college beyond posing as a layperson's Dorothy Parker and possibly killing my liver.

I was aware of Mark's presence on the campus. Further, I was aware that we were complete opposites. I was argumentative concerning causes I believed worthy while Mark was boisterous, pompous and crude, often just for the pure joy of it. He was an adrenaline junky who lived life on the edge, literally— cliff diving and base jumping with a bunch of other jocky numbskulls. He was considered a catch by way of athleticism and good looks, but those qualities rarely softened the blows his vile tongue, delivered in that ridiculous hick-accent, regardless of his audience. Often, he'd offend and be gone before his initial charm had even worn thin and his barb had quite sunk in. As for his studies, he had no love for any subjects, only a passion for fast-tracking his way to a quick buck. Come to think of it, he was perfect for Tatum.

Mark received his degree in chemistry. I suspect his major was supported in part by his ability to cut marijuana and PCP to create his own designer "super-weed" that made his frat house's parties the hottest ticket on campus. After graduation, someone hired him and let him play with chemicals for a living and I could not help but wonder about the coincidence of his becoming gainfully employed by a government-affiliated agency mere months before the United States experienced one hell of an anthrax scare. But that's just me being a smart-ass. I hope. How Mark and I came to be married is a ridiculously simple and entirely unromantic story: I got knocked up.

Seven years before I died, I crashed a USC reunion for what should have been my graduating class. I was in town anyway to do an interview for an article I was writing for the painfully dull magazine I was working for. Ironically, I'd decided to attend the reunion at the encouragement of my good old buddy, Tate. Then, of course, she got a few drinks in her and left with a nerd-turned-heavily-invested-rocket-scientist—talk about foreshadowing—so I headed off to the hotel bar to get a sandwich. I only made it to the elevator where I bumped into Mark, who'd apparently, over the course of the three-day event, already exhausted his supply of graduating class pussy and was fleeing the glaring eyes of his conquests and more importantly, their husbands. We ended up back in his room, where we drank ourselves stupid and talked about old times that we never shared.

We had sex for our own reasons; Mark because he fucked everything, and me because I was desperate to prove to myself that I wasn't the cold, loveless bitch I'd been accused of being by a former boy who was a friend, but never made it to actual boyfriend. None of them did. I wanted to believe I was capable of entering into a relationship, even if only for a single night. I wanted to discredit other possible reasons niggling in the back of my mind that could also account for my inability to have a relationship with a man.

Getting pregnant via the "quickie" certainly did change my life, but it did not change my heart's growing desire for clarity regarding my sexuality. I was confused as hell. To my utter astonishment, Mark wanted his child and he claimed to want me. We married weeks later in a courtroom in Hoboken and lived unhappily ever after.

Mark went on to climb the ladder of success, getting by on a wink and a smile and whatever brain cells he had left over from his college days, while I did whatever freelance work I could get without straying outside my very narrow parameters. Aside from being pregnant and sick and unfamiliar with my new surroundings, I had to contend with Mark's paranoid, possessive ways.

To Mark, a marriage certificate seemed only to be a certificate of ownership. Mark was the product of another dysfunctional marriage, sibling to two sisters and three brothers, all either divorced or with children out of wedlock. To Mark, marriage and family was another symbol of success. He'd make weekly long-distance phone calls to his father—who was just like him—

to brag about his stylish little family and house, important job and healthy income level. The conversations were a lot of hot air and atta-boys. Like father, like son.

Mark interrogated me about everywhere I went and anyone I talked to. I'd managed to hit enough psychology classes to know that Mark's personality exemplified a classic case of insecurity. He was blatantly unhappy with our marriage and I knew I was solely to blame. I didn't know how to love him. I was also miserable, but I assumed it was God's retribution for my inability to love my husband. I was in a complete downward spiral of depression until my daughter entered into this world.

I wanted to set a good, loving example for my daughter, but our household did anything but demonstrate that. We'd even get into shoving matches, which isn't cool, and over time he'd toss in a slap. I was a stranger in my own home and a victim of my own fears—I didn't want to disappoint my mother, was afraid of raising a child alone, afraid of failing Bella financially—the list goes on. When I made the decision to leave Mark, my goal was to be out by Bella's third birthday; instead we were gone two days after her second birthday. Blame it on the lawn.

From a work standpoint, Mark was a wannabe mad scientist. He'd bring stuff home and play with "potions" to the degree that one bathroom in our two-bed, two-bath home had been deemed "the laboratory," complete with a deadbolt on the inside and outside of the door. At work, his unit was designing a unique bug repellent for our troops in Iraq. The product could be incorporated into the fibers of their battle uniforms, worn over the long term without harming the wearer, and washed repeatedly without losing its effectiveness.

It was while Mark was working on this project that he made an accidental discovery, thereby spawning an elaborate home pet project that he supplemented by liberally "borrowing" chemicals from work and smuggling them home in stainless steel thermoses. He swore he was onto "the next big thing" and announced one day that he was going to test it on our lawn—the lawn where his daughter played daily. I pitched a five-star fit.

"Just how in hell do you suppose any product ever hits the shelf if it's not tested, hmm?" He stood in front of his makeshift laboratory door like a protective sentry. "How stupid can you be?"

"Deal with it at work. They'll know what to do with it."

"And share credit with the goddamned company? Won't they think it's a little funny that I have all the chemicals in my possession that I just happen to work with in the government lab? Are you fucking brainless or what?"

"Tell them you made it during your lunch hour—maybe they'll test it out and figure you're onto something and give you a great big promotion."

"A *promotion?* This thing could be worth millions to groundskeepers everywhere and you want me to hand it over to my fucking boss? Maybe you'd like me to put a big old bow on it, huh?"

I lowered my gaze, spoke with conviction. "You experiment with anything in this house and so help me God, I'll contact every government agency with an acronym and get them on the case, but not before I make an anonymous call to your company to turn you in."

He glared at me. I held tight to his look, hoping he wouldn't notice my trembling.

"That's fine," he calmly said, folding his arms across his chest. He coolly leaned against the bathroom door and gave me his best asshole grin. "You'll go right down with me."

Maybe he had a point. Still, I tried my best hand at appearing steely strong.

I responded with my best sarcasm. "Yeah, because I slipped past security and stole materials from your lab, right? You're not licensed to have such things in your possession. It shouldn't even be in our house let alone around our daughter."

I could tell he'd considered knocking me on my ass; I could also tell he was trying to figure out if I had the nerve to carry out my threat. I stood firm, didn't flinch. I sure as hell didn't want his Mr. Wizard-meddling to make Bella sick or worse.

We didn't speak of it again. For months we continued to live and work; together, yet worlds apart.

On one unseasonably warm January day shortly after Bella's second birthday, she whined until I agreed to let her take her best gift, a hamster named Brownie, into the backyard so he could play. I read a magazine while she played nearby, but only half an hour into our outing, she came to me in tears, gingerly holding her beloved Brownie, who'd been happily nuzzling his furry face in the grass only minutes before. She handed me the limp rodent and I poked and prodded the poor pudgy creature, puzzled about its sudden demise. I dropped onto the lawn and cradled my sobbing daughter in my arms. I was somewhere in the midst of those comforting efforts when the smell hit me. It fell somewhere between the smell of car wax and chlorine.

I scooped up Bella and ran with her into the house where I stripped her clothing off and dunked her into an impromptu bath I'd hurriedly drawn in the kitchen sink. She cried the entire time while I scrubbed her pink, trying to rid her of some toxin I could not see, only smell. Frantically, I called the poison—control center, but they were unable to help me given my nearly absent description. They assured me that since Bella wasn't suffering any outward adverse affects, I should only observe her for the next few hours. Further, they suggested, the hamster could very well have been sick and nothing more.

Dissatisfied, I called the neighborhood librarian and was given two telephone numbers. The first was for the EPA in Washington, D.C. The second was for an environmental researcher and activist in New York. I wanted answers that day. I chose door number two.

I'd never really spent any time in the city, had never caught a train or a subway. I called a cab and paid a fortune for a ride to a university near Greenwich Village. Armed with a two-year-old, a sippy cup and a dead hamster, I tracked down Mara Rossi. That was five years, eleven months, twenty days and four hours before I died.

Chapter 12

Five years, eleven months, twenty days and four hours before I died.

I entered her tiny office, which was tucked beneath the stairwell. I suspected it was actually a converted broom closet. Mara Rossi's features were partially hidden by tousled wisps of dark hair that framed her face, and although she was lean and actually fairly tall, the massive stacks of manila folders piled before her practically dwarfed her as she stood behind the desk.

She startled slightly upon my entrance and lifted only her eyes to see me, gazing over the tops of her dark-rimmed reading glasses. Nervous, not to mention breathless from having carried a sleeping child up four flights of stairs, I approached Ms. Rossi without a word and plunked the paper sack onto her cluttered desk. She stared blankly at me.

After I'd caught my breath, I briefly explained who I was

and what I wanted and she listened without interrupting. When I finished, she removed her glasses and hesitantly peeked into the sack.

"You've actually brought me a rodent. Pleasant."

It seemed like a rather bitchy thing to say. Obviously I was distraught and had traveled a little distance to stand in her doorway, where I stood slightly swaying in place so that my daughter might remain sleeping. I found Ms. Rossi's demeanor chilly, and it appeared to me that she believed I was off my rocker. I was instantly put off.

"Look—do I need to go somewhere else? If so just tell me where and I'll take my rodent and get out of your space."

She didn't react to my harshness. Instead, she wrote something down on a sticky note and pressed it onto the hamster-bag. With a calmness that was downright annoying and using a bored-sounding, doctoral tone, she began her line of questioning.

"Has the child developed any kind redness, rash or itchiness?"

"No. I checked her over real good in the cab."

"Any blisters, crusts, scales…"

I shook my head no.

"Nausea, vomiting, dysuria or hematuria?"

"No, no and I don't know what those last two are."

"Has she had any change in her urinary habits?"

"Not that I know of."

She jotted a few notes. "Naturally, if her behavior or physical appearance changes during the night, you'll take her to the closest ER."

"Naturally." I ducked my head, tried to make eye contact with the woman hunched over her notes. "Can you help me? Can you tell me what's on that lawn?"

"I don't know. It depends."

"On what?"

"Time and resources." She capped her pen and dropped it next to the hamster bag, leaned across her desk and gave me her full attention. "This is a nonprofit organization. For an overly generous tax write-off and name affiliation, the university affords me these luxurious quarters—" She waved her hand around the tiny, shadowy room and smirked, "—and though the science labs are cutting edge, the professors donate their time and resources based on their schedule and budget, both of which are tight. I have one intern. My own salary is practically nonexistent. Do I paint a picture you can understand here?"

I was embarrassed and angry at the same time. I could tell she'd sized me up—dark denim jeans, Ralph Lauren sweater and Coach baby bag—and had me figured as a pristine, yuppie wife with a penchant toward dramatics. How was she to know it was all window dressing designed by Mark for his version of a perfect wife? I tried to remain calm.

"I just want to know if my daughter has been exposed to anything harmful. Is that so bad?"

"And I'm in the business of exposing harmful pesticides and the companies behind them. Speaking of which, if her arms fall off in the middle of the night, what chemical company will you and the hubby be seeking punitive damages from?"

I stared at her, blinked in disbelief and then spun around to make a record-fast exit.

For such a cluttered room and considering the mile-high paperwork that practically caged her behind her desk, Ms. Rossi made an equally world—fast trek to the door to stop me from leaving. I wish I'd actually seen it; I had a feeling she'd have rivaled Jackie Joyner-Kersee with her amazing jump over that mess.

"I'm sorry—that was a fucking morbid thing to say," she told me. Mara Rossi looked genuinely regretful, although she was having great difficulty looking me in the eye. She stumbled on, "Maybe I've been here too long. My manners are lacking."

"So is your humanity," I coldly told her.

She shrugged. "I deserve that." She patted the pockets of her lab coat and finally produced a business card that she handed to me. "Here's my info. I'll need a number where I can reach you."

"I—I can't." It was my turn to stammer. I tried to look into her deep brown eyes, which seemed sincere, despite her earlier meanness. I was compelled to level with her at the risk of implicating myself. I felt I had no choice. "My…husband is a professional tinkerer. He's made a little lab in our house and now he's working on a pesticide of sorts."

She looked frustrated. "You know that's illegal on so many levels."

"I do. I know that." I swallowed hard. "I don't have a good number to be reached at. He'd be very angry if he knew I was here." I glanced at my watch. "I have to go. He'll be home in three hours. I'll call you soon about this."

The longer I'd stood there, the heavier Bella had gotten. I felt her stir in my arms and I was nervous or scared, though I couldn't be sure of what. I started toward the stairs, calling softly to the woman as I went. "I'd like to know as quickly as possible. I'll call you soon."

I heard her ask if I was okay, but I did not answer her. In truth I wasn't okay. Suddenly all my superficial worries seemed to vanish. How dare I risk my child's physical health when I knew full well that Mark had been playing with dangerous stuff in that bathroom for years—never mind the damage I was sure we'd inflicted on her emotional health from our escalating violent arguments. I wanted to cry forever. Instead, I caught a cab and comforted my confused daughter when she awoke to the flickering neon inside the Holland Tunnel on our way back to New Jersey.

Chapter 13

Mark and Tatie's fancy new shed had a dark interior thanks to the sheets of plywood that covered every window of the small building. The only light was an occasional streak that managed its way in between the warped edges where the sheets butted up against each other. In any other neighborhood except this one, the cops would have been all over it to see if there was marijuana growing inside or even a meth lab.

Trinidad waved his hand through the air and caught the freely swinging bare lightbulb that dangled from the ceiling. He screwed it in tightly, causing forty watts of barely-there light to shower the place. I could see perfectly well in the dark, so I figured it was his intention to have a spotlight. I moved in for a closer look.

Several rows of burlap bags stamped with a GreenSafe logo lined the walls. I thumped my bare toe against one and it felt solid, probably one hundred pounds. I was quickly forming notions about what they contained.

"Oh no…" I moved around the place, which smelled of chlorine and grass seed.

Trinidad was fascinated with something altogether different and I went to join him. He pulled a DVD out of a crate of empty bags and located a little DVD-TV combo player. He powered it up and slid the disk into the tray. It was a professionally produced pitch piece that resembled a late-night infomercial, starring—of course—my husband.

"Imagine being able to enjoy your club golf grounds without the worry and bother of expensive upkeep. Imagine smooth lawns as far as you can see that need trimming only twice a year. Imagine divots that virtually replace themselves within twelve hours. Can you imagine the ease of pest-free greens? Can you imagine a solution for common bugs, moles, gophers and other nuisance animals that regularly wreak havoc on greens, costing hundreds of thousands of dollars annually for golf organizations?"

Mark moseyed past a tremendous green screen as it flashed images of poorly kept grounds and a course owner wincing at his quarterly bill from his greenkeeper. It was exaggerated and cheesy at best.

"When you are able to reduce the outrageous expense of manpower and costly chemicals to treat your course, fees are reduced and profit margins increase. Golf courses throughout the world have had to deal with the issue of keeping their greens, fairways and rough in the best possible condition throughout the playing season, seasonally or year round. Maintaining good and playable grounds includes pest control, general grounds maintenance and divot repair. These factors have been the nemesis of groundkeepers worldwide. I always say, the golf greens are the most valuable real estate on the golf course…"

The pieces were rapidly clicking into place, and even dead, my knees felt wobbly. I slowly slunk to the floor in front of the small set.

New images flooded the screen—happy course owners, lovely, lush lawns…

"GreenSafe will revolutionize greenway upkeep worldwide. Its patented formula three-step system literally dwarfs grass at the proper

height for greens, fairways, and roughs, keeping it a nice, even height,
consistently across the course, all year long. GreenSafe has taken away
the need for chemical spraying…"

I glanced at Trinidad who was watching me, awaiting my
reaction. I had questions, and lots of them.

"GreenSafe makes it possible to cut greens twice a year. GreenSafe
has eliminated the need for resodding and repairing grounds."

Onscreen, Mark came to a stop and leaned against a park
bench situated in front of the slide show. He was the recipe for
down-home, everyday guy believability. He struck a handsome
pose and gave the camera his best toothy smile.

"So, now that GreenSafe has eliminated every greenkeeper's
nightmares, whatever are you going to do with all your leftover
money? The only thing we didn't put in this formula was a way to fish
your golf ball out of the pond. Well, there's always the next formula."

I turned to Trinidad, horrified. "He actually did intend to
kill me, didn't he?" I barreled ahead with my summation. "Did
he need some kid-props to stage his 'perfect' life?" I hooked air
quotes, growing as angry as I possibly could. "Was he afraid my
sexuality would taint his reputation, or that somebody in the
media would discover I'd been his favorite punching bag? My
guess is that none of that would set too well with his good-guy
image."

I would have been in tears if it was possible.

"Where did he get the startup money? From Tatie?" But I
could have answered my question before I even finished asking
it. Life insurance. Mine. Trinidad only solemnly nodded. "He
could have cashed it out! I told him I wouldn't say anything
about any of it. I kept my end of the bargain, that rotten bastard!"

Chapter 14

Five years, eight months, twelve days and eight hours before I died.
I finally called Mara Rossi eight days after dropping off the hamster. I got her intern and left word that I was in town and requested that Mara meet me. I failed to mention that I'd been in town for nearly a week. I'd already staked out a decent and cheap coffee shop not far from my dive of a hotel on MacDougal Street. Without the slightest confirmation that the woman had even gotten my message, I buckled Bella in a flimsy portable stroller and started for The Bean Cup an hour ahead of the appointment time. I took a stool at the window counter. She showed up right on the button.

Mara grabbed coffee and slid onto the stool next to me and mouthed "Hello" when she saw my sleeping child.

"S'okay," I told her. "She's a heavy sleeper." The midday sun shone hazily through the steamy shop windows. From behind plate-sized sunglasses, I watched her sip from a steaming mug and I waited for her to settle, trying my best to not to launch into a full-fledged interrogation. I made preliminary niceties. "Thanks for meeting me."

"Well, I have to say that was my first time ordering an autopsy on a hamster." She removed her glasses and shoved them on top of her head. "That little guy have a name?"

"Brownie." My sunglasses afforded me the guilty luxury of carefully studying her. She wore faded jeans and a drab army-style jacket. A black scarf gave her look some polish, but overall she seemed far less rigid than she had in her office. She looked softer, and something I dared not even to consider—though I'd be blind not to notice—Mara Rossi was pretty in a sturdy way.

"Well then, your pal Brownie died as a result of idiopathic pulmonary fibrosis."

When I asked what that meant, I could tell she was trying to choose her words carefully to avoid making me feel absolutely dumb—particularly in light of the poor start we'd gotten off to a week earlier.

"It's a cluster of lung nodules—tumors—that had grown so large, they literally suffocated the poor thing."

"Caused by the pesticide?"

"It's called idiopathic, which means that there's no clear cause, unfortunately."

"Idiopathic," I echoed and softly smirked. "I thought you were referring to my husband."

She shot me a fleeting smile before continuing. "Pulmonary fibrosis is generally caused by inhaled contaminants, like with asbestos and such. But sometimes it just can't be pinpointed. It can be anything—exposure to radiation, medications, something bacterial, animal, or fungal. And then there are environmental agents, which could include your pesticide."

"I just want to know if it could harm my daughter."

"I take it you haven't noticed any of the symptoms we discussed, particularly shortness of breath or coughing?"

"No, not at all."

"Chances are she's fine. Obviously the hamster's lungs are much smaller than a child's, which increase the animal's risk."

She shrugged, took another careful sip of her steaming coffee. "Also, keep in mind it's not out of the question that this was a preexisting condition with Brownie. My guess is that it'd be nearly impossible to sustain that kind of injury to the lungs after only a half-hour outdoors. I've seen cases where lab mice were given an outlandish concentration of chemicals for weeks and didn't develop the nodules that your hamster had." She took another sip, and almost under her breath added, "I hate it when they experiment on animals."

"So you're telling me this could be entirely circumstantial— that Brownie may already have been on the fast track to death from natural causes?"

"Possibly. Unless you're going to tell me that Brownie was a lifelong smoker." She smiled, but I didn't. Mara continued. "There's an extremely remote chance—and I emphasize extremely—that he could have been exposed to an environmental agent that caused tumor generation to literally replicate itself on the spot until he smothered to death. But that would be fast. I'd hate like hell to think there's something out there that could do that."

"Bottom line?"

She shrugged. "I'd say somewhere between the two. Unhealthy pet with scarred lungs and exposure to chemicals, all of which pushed the poor critter right over the edge. Of course, you can always take the chemical to a government lab and let them check it out. No, never mind—don't touch the stuff, I've got an EPA whistleblower's hotline number." Mara arched an eyebrow and glanced in Bella's direction. "Of course, that will pretty much end your marriage, I'll warn you."

My tone was noticeably warbled. "That's no longer a concern."

My gaze wandered out the window, toward a woman and her child taking a carefree walk. Completely absorbed in private misery, I flinched at Mara's surprising touch to my cheek. Without words, she gently removed my sunglasses, revealing my dandy of a bruised eye that had turned green in its gory final stage. I forced myself to look into her eyes, and we stayed like that for several moments while I allowed her to satisfy her curiosity. When I slid my glasses back in place she did not stop me.

"My advice is to call the EPA, but not before you get the hell out of that house."

"I am out," I quietly assured her.

Bella stirred a little in her stroller and for a moment I thought she would wake up. I tucked her favorite blanket around her little shoulders and waited, but she still slept.

"I've been in the neighborhood all week, actually."

"And this is the first time you've tried to contact me?"

I couldn't be sure if she was surprised or insulted.

"Bella seemed okay. Besides, I know you're busy, a point made quite clear to me upon our initial meeting by your cluttered desk and…your impatience." But my words were void of contempt.

"Where are you staying?"

"Hotel on MacDougal."

"That place is a dive."

I smiled. "Yeah, well they don't charge dive prices."

"Got family here? Any money?"

I shook my head on both counts. "I'm getting a hold of my parents in Iowa this afternoon."

"Will they help?"

I forced a smile. "Are you kidding? I can't tell you how much joy it will bring them to tell me how I've screwed up my life. Again."

We were quiet.

"I'm sorry I can't be more helpful about Brownie. Further testing is expensive and I've used up all my pro bono with everyone I know." She hesitated only a moment before adding, "Wish I had a divorce lawyer who owed me a favor."

I thanked Mara kindly and left her there. I felt her watching me through the storefront window as I pushed my daughter's stroller slowly down the sidewalk.

Back at Roach-Hotel, I surveyed the meager belongings I'd scrounged together before hastily leaving home. Everything was Bella's, save for a handful of items. Though we enjoyed a fairly reasonable income, Mark had canceled my ATM card and

I had only paid for one more night's stay. Also, Mark had our only cell phone—he claimed the home phone was my phone—and the hotel didn't have lines in its rooms.

Bella was waking up and I knew she'd want to be fed. I felt guilty for having spent five bucks on coffee, but that was before I'd realized my credit card had also been canceled. I had eight dollars cash to my name, which I figured I'd offer the front desk clerk in exchange for a five-minute call to Iowa. My parents could probably wire me a few bucks to buy a plane ticket to Des Moines by morning. Mama would pick me up and lecture me all the way back to Willow Creek, not out of spite, but because that's what Catholic mothers do. Thinking about it made me consider going back to Mark and begging forgiveness. That insane idea dissipated when I heard a knock on my door. I wondered how things could possibly get worse.

"Great," I muttered to my sleeping child as I strained to peek through the worthless, cloudy peephole. "Maybe that's my mugging."

It was Mara Rossi.

Chapter 15

There was a commotion under the big top and I hurriedly left Mark's shed and headed outside to investigate. I ducked under the canopy in time to hear Tatum let out an ear-piercing scream. A petting zoo goose was literally goosing the mistress of the house, and she was not displaying a splendid sense of humor about it.

She called for Mark, who was nowhere to be found, and I could not help but smile as I watched an old fellow dressed in a beige knobby sweater and tweed slacks break from his patrician crowd and stage an only moderately successful intervention. A caterer joined in and together they eventually pried the poor creature's jaws open, releasing the distressed damsel. Bella wore an ashamed smile on her lips that she could not stifle. The children stood quietly by watching the display, which topped any amusement the party organizers could have concocted.

Then another service person approached my little daughter and placed a vented cardboard box on the ground before her. She quickly scanned the enclosed card and her face lit up.

"It's from Mama Mara!"

Cooper was at her side in an instant. Tatum was still recovering from her goosing, but her curiosity was also visibly piqued. Brushing the dirt off her unseasonable white cocktail dress, she moved closer into the circle of kids and adults to get a better look. I jogged over and climbed right on top of the sturdy cake table situated nearby. It was the best view in the house and would have been considered entirely inappropriate in my living years.

Bella untied the lavish satin bow on top and squealed with sheer delight. Her head, hands, arms, and then almost her entire body disappeared into the box, and when she came up again, she was holding a squirmy West Highland Terrier puppy.

"It's McDuff!" She loudly proclaimed. "Cooper—it's *McDuff!*"

Everyone wore polite smiles but looked utterly puzzled— everyone but two very excited children and a dead woman. We got it.

Mara and I had promised Bella and Cooper a Westie puppy. Ideally, the four of us would have picked it out together right after the holiday. Of course, that was before I'd gone and got myself killed and ruined everyone's lives.

Instead, sweet Mara had obviously selected a puppy identical to one in the kids' favorite Christmas book, *McDuff's Christmas*. McDuff was the dog whose spirited antics always landed him in the doghouse and whose hilarious adventures had our kids rolling on the floor with laughter. It was a great coincidence in our favor that the kids' doctor had recommended a Westie, claiming that the dog was a minimal risk to most allergic and asthmatic children. Cooper's condition, though improved over the years, affected even the most seemingly insignificant decisions.

Now McDuff was three—dimensional and obviously every bit as lively as his alter ego and already being well—loved by his new young owners. It was touching enough that I'd have been suffering from full onset happy weepiness had I been alive. I thought of Mara and pictured her in New York, alone in the home that should contain two children and a dog, at least.

I scanned the crowd for Trinidad and nearly leapt out of my ethereal skin to discover he was standing on the tabletop directly behind me. I'd been preoccupied by random small children eyeing me with great curiosity as I stood on the table above them all.

"So, why is it some of these children can see us and others cannot?"

A little girl made her way over to the edge of our makeshift pedestal and smiled up at us. She waved. I forced a tiny smile and waved back. Being dead was truly a trip.

"Like the animals, children are pure, but even they lose their ability to see us around eight years old or so." He wriggled his eyebrows at them in an uncharacteristic playful action. "Haven't you ever wondered why children outgrow their imaginary friends?"

No, I had not. Any further questions from me were deferred when I caught wind of Tatum off to the side, animatedly chastising Mark. Clearly, she was horrified by the late-delivered gift. I scooted off the tabletop and went in for a better listen.

"How in the hell did you let this happen?" she screeched in a whisper so loud, why did she bother at all. "Don't you have any control over your own children whatsoever?"

"Calm down, Tatie." Mark displayed more patience than I'd ever witnessed out of him when we were together. Apparently he'd just needed a bigger bully than he was. That, or perhaps he really loved her. For the record, I would not have suffered any anguish over these Mark-love-notions had I been alive. He killed me, after all. He rubbed her arms, kissed her cheek, whispered, "Go change. I'll get you a drink."

"Children are one thing, but I'll be damned if I'm keeping a kennel, too."

"We'll discuss it later."

No one noticed Tatum's exit. All eyes were focused on the children and their new, much-adored puppy.

I felt Trinidad behind me before I saw him.

"Trini, why am I here? Why are my children here?" I couldn't feel any true sadness or deep pain, so it confused me when I heard my own voice break. "They should be at home with their mother."

Chapter 16

Five years, eight months, twelve days and five hours before I died.
"I could never be a mother," Mara quietly said.

I stood on the landing in the narrow hallway outside 4E in a brownstone apartment building with a toddler balanced on my hip. Mara shoved three keys into three locks in record fast succession and kneed the door open. It swung wide and we made our entrance juggling armloads of everything I had. She carried our suitcase and the collapsible stroller, chores which appeared highly uncharacteristic for her; I had my child on one side and hauled an oversized mom-bag over my opposite shoulder. Bella held fast to her blanket and had hardly uttered a peep the entire stroller ride to the apartment or the subsequent walk up four floors. She barely took her eyes off Mara, and her little head was on a swivel, craning to see the woman each time I pushed her stroller too far ahead or if we got behind—kid was born a quiet observer.

"What makes you say that?" I asked a little out of breath from the steep walk up.

She hesitated only a moment, shrugged. "Don't know. I just can't see it."

"I used to feel the same way. Then Bella came along and now I can't imagine life without her."

I was glad for the temporary cover of the hallway darkness, and I lingered there a moment before making my entrance. "You know, you didn't have to make us your personal charity case."

She heaved my suitcase through the door and set it aside. "I couldn't very well send you back to that place now, could I?"

"You could have done nothing at all."

"No. I couldn't have." She felt along the wall for a switch. "Humans have a certain amount of responsibility to one another."

"It would be nice if that was true." It was too quiet. I set my bag down the same time she found the switch. Artistically placed light fixtures lined the hallway and bathed the apartment in a soft glow, affording me a look at her place for the first time. It was amazing. I only mumbled, "Whoa."

"What?" Mara set about the place, turning on more lights.

Her tennis shoes made a squeaking sound on the hardwood floors. She shrugged off her coat and reached her hand out for mine, but I didn't surrender it right away. I was too busy taking in the deep green walls with perfect white chair rails and built-in mahogany cabinets chock full of books. Her apartment, though small, was as beautiful as anything I'd seen in a home magazine. It was a true showplace. I guess I wouldn't have figured it from the woman in jeans and a crew neck sweatshirt who didn't appear to have an ounce of pretentiousness in her entire body.

At the same time I saw the beauty of the apartment, I also saw breakable glass, sharp edges, exposed outlets and clean walls free of even the tiniest accidental crayon mark—call it mom-goggles.

Mara edged closer to me as I stood in the center of the floor. I took a cautionary step away from her before I could stop myself, and then I felt foolish.

"What is it?"

"Money in nonprofit must seriously rock," I said at last. I set my bag down, careful not to touch anything but the floor with it. Then upon noting wood floors polished to a near-glare, I considered that perhaps I should set my bag on a rug.

"I was a lawyer before I was an activist."

"Why'd you give it up?"

"I began to develop an aversion to garlic and crucifixes." I'd become focused on her in her own surroundings and she thought I didn't get her joke. She moved to clarify herself. "Bunch of bloodsuckers."

"You must have got a heck of a severance package."

A smiled touched her lips before she launched into an abbreviated tour. "The kitchen and living room are that way." She motioned for me to follow her down the long, narrow hallway. "This is the bathroom, not really spacious." She nodded toward French doors at the very end. "That's my little room, and this is my very little room." She stepped inside a converted office of sorts with a desk, more bookcases and a couch.

"It folds out." She must have taken my silence as disapproval because she added, "Is it okay?"

Embarrassed, I nodded. "It's more than okay. I appreciate it. I promise we'll be out of here in a few days."

Bella had grown heavy and apparently bored, and was struggling to get out of my arms. I pried her out of her little coat and finally let her go. I figured I'd be chasing her down the hallway in a split second, dodging glass and pricey antiques. Instead, she took a few steps forward and leaned against the doorway of the small room. She pointed a tiny, pudgy finger into the air and said, "Moon."

My gaze followed her finger, and sure enough there was a moon on the ceiling along with a smattering of stars painted so cleverly they looked shiny, almost three—dimensional. It was actually wonderful.

Bella, who was practically born talking plainly, turned back to Mara and quietly informed her, "Cow jumped over the moon."

Mara blinked and furrowed her brow. "Yeah, I think I

remember that."

"The dish ran away with the spoon." Then Bella, apparently inspired by the mere mention of the eating utensils, looked thoughtful. I already knew what was going on in her head. She was long overdue for dinner and confirmed my suspicion. "Do you have ohs?"

Mara hesitated a moment and then knelt to my child's level. She looked thoroughly confused, but spoke to her without the baby-talk words that so many adults use with small children. "What are ohs?"

Bella put her hands together to form a circle.

"Cheerios," I interpreted. "I probably have some in my bag. Can you keep an eye on her for a sec? There's a lot of…I just don't want her to accidentally break—"

"How about I make us something to eat. Are you hungry? I'm starving."

After the emotional day—check that—week I'd had, food was honestly the last thing on my mind.

Mara practically sprinted toward the kitchen. She called behind her, "Make yourself at home."

For dinner, Mara fed us her own version of "ohs"—round cheese-stuffed tortellini, sauce and a nice, crusty loaf of bread. Mark refused all Italian food, so pasta was a new experience to my kid. Mara had cleverly served her pasta bare and her sauce on the side as dip, and just like that dinner had become an event for Bella. I was amazed that she actually tried it, and when she loved it, I pegged her to be more like my people than Marks's. Childish of me, I know.

Mara refused my offer to help clean up afterward. Bella and I retreated to our room, and by the time I heard Mara's footsteps in the hallway my daughter was bathed, powdered, pajama'd and asleep on the foldout bed. Mara paused in the hallway and poked her head into our little room.

"You good?"

"Some of us are even better than others." I motioned toward my sleeping child.

"That was quick," she whispered. "Does she always go down that easily?"

"Mostly. She went pretty quickly tonight, though."

I was suddenly self-conscious when I felt Mara looking at my freshly scrubbed, bruised face. I purposely tipped my head slightly forward, causing a thick wave of long bangs to fall across my bruise. I tucked the blanket around my daughter and brushed soft, curly hair out of her eyelashes. "She was pretty focused on your moon and stars action on the ceiling there. It's beautiful."

"I can't take any credit for it. My ex is an artist."

"Well, he certainly created a kid's Sistine Chapel."

Mara smiled and nodded. "Yeah, she did."

That night I fell asleep pondering her simple response. I couldn't explain why it relieved me to learn that she'd been involved with a woman. I'd sensed that much from her, but my instincts about most everything else had failed me for nearly three years. Therefore, I admit I'd fished for confirmation of her orientation, and for what reason, well, I certainly could not explain that either.

Chapter 17

"You should rest."

Trinidad's soothing voice came from the twin bed next to mine. It was after midnight and we were sharing one of the ridiculously frilly guest suites.

My children were both bedded down in Bella's room along with their new puppy, and I'd lingered until long after they were all asleep. It took them longer than usual to wind down, and I could tell it was the combination of being excited about having McDuff and me making a surprise appearance in their lives. I hoped I'd be around for a few days. I seemed to be on an otherworldly timetable that I wasn't privy to.

After I was sure they were asleep, a very kind, albeit dead, gentleman showed me to our guest suite. The nice old fellow went so far as to turn back the covers and poured me a cup of hot tea—or so he proclaimed it to be. I felt neither its heat, nor could I taste its flavor. I was getting used to it by now. I wondered how so many Deads came to be living in a relatively new neighborhood.

"I'm not tired and besides, why bother with rest?" I raised my head slightly and looked across the beds at my companion. "Seriously—think we'll be dead tired?"

"Funny," he mumbled.

I dropped my head back against the pillow, and employed my girly, sarcastic voice. "Oh, this lack of sleep is killing me."

He raised his head up long enough to make brief eye contact with me. "It's pointless to lie here and worry about things over which you have no control."

"It's as impossible to be truly worried as it is to be truly tired." I sighed and rolled his words back through my brain. "And if I have no control over anything, why did you bring me here?"

"Laney…"

"I know—you can't talk to me about that." I slowly counted to twenty and still I felt like moving around. "Trini?"

"Yes?"

"How did he afford this societal circus-life? The life insurance wasn't that much and the product hasn't even hit the market yet."

"I can't talk to you about that." He heard me sigh and figured I would begin my protest so he changed the subject. "Why don't you tell me about your last day alive?"

"Well, I took a flight on a small plane piloted by my ex-husband which, I think we can both agree, was clearly a bad idea."

"Also, he's clearly not your ex," he corrected, prompting a deeper, more dramatic sigh out of me. Trinidad deferred another one of my rants with his diversionary tactics—tactics I was on to, by the way.

He said, "Tell me what happened before that."

"Okay, before that," I said, growing quiet and thoughtful. "Mark called out of the blue. He said he was ready to sign the divorce papers after all, slightly ahead of our agreed upon time. Back before I knew he was going to kill me for my silence and a wad of insurance money, I had enjoyed some great relief that he wanted to speed up the process because I obviously didn't want to stay married to Mark. And though you seem to think I'm a terrible person for having done so, you should know that not divorcing wasn't my choice."

"People always have a choice—the right one and the wrong one."

"You are so righteous." I rose up on my elbows and looked across the dark bedroom. "You have no idea what I went through. Mark threatened to tie me up in a custody battle over Bella if I tried to divorce him. It was complicated, and not that you think I have anyone's best interest at heart, but I didn't want to risk having to share custody of the kids with that asshole-prick. So sue me."

Trinidad also rose up on his elbows and looked right back at me. "Of course, because being dead and leaving your kids with a man of questionable integrity and a perfect stranger is such a better alternative."

"Like I planned to get killed." I fell back against the pillow and sighed as loudly as I could. "Jesus Christ."

I could practically feel him cringe from across the room. I heard the sheets rustle as he lay back down and settled in. After several minutes of silence, I figured Trinidad was deep in meditation and though I figured I was probably talking to no one, maybe I just wanted to hear my own side of the story again.

"Years ago, Mark got into some trouble at work and it looked like they were taking him to court. Then there was me, threatening to turn him in for being some kind of mad chemist. I did some research, came up with all the right terms for every violation he'd committed. I accused him of everything from groundwater poisoning to theft."

Trinidad softly interjected, "Why didn't you follow through with it?"

"Mark's attorney, Nelson—I saw him in the study today—he advised Mark about the statute of limitations and about a bunch of hang-ups the court has with spouses testifying against each other. Without my testimony, there'd be no case."

It seemed like a valid argument during the days Mara and I mulled it to death. It was a major ethics hot button in our home, but protecting the children won out every time. Ultimately, we'd turned our backs on the larger issue. What seemed like the wisest decision at the time had now quickly lost its luster.

I continued. "Mark said that if I divorced him, he'd easily take custody of Bella away from two women. He didn't know I was pregnant with my son. He said he would tie us up in legal hell, and in the meantime he'd still have half-time custody of Bella until permanent custody was decided by a judge. But, if I agreed not to file for a divorce right away, he'd be ensured some legal protection, and for that he was willing to leave us all alone."

I looked at Trinidad, who was listening patiently. "You have no idea what it was like to live with him. I couldn't do that to my children. Not even on a half-time basis."

"So you avoided sharing custody of your children by way of risking neighborhoods and the individuals and animals that might come into contact with an illegally produced product?"

"You make it sound like he was running a meth lab."

"Are you defending him or making excuses for yourself? You had direct knowledge and you didn't even risk punishment, and that's probably the worst crime of all. People are inherently programmed to do what's right." He sighed and his voice went soft, and I don't believe he was actually speaking to me when he added, "So why don't they? The Creator always defends those whose intentions are true and good."

"My intentions were true and good. I was afraid."

Once again Trinidad's tone gathered steam as he chastised me. "People are afraid of war. They're afraid of not being able to feed their children. People are afraid of dying alone or watching their children die—they are *not* afraid of losing custody of their children to lying imbeciles who make idle threats." He practically spat the last words, but he wasn't finished yet. "*You* made yourself a victim and you gladly accepted your role, and that is something only a real pansy-ass angel would do, frankly."

Any guilt those words might have inspired in me was

overshadowed by my surprise at hearing a swear word tumble from Trinidad's virginal lips. He'd echoed my earlier sentiments with brilliant sarcasm, nicely too, if I did say so myself.

"I thought we weren't angels." I lifted my head back up to see my companion. He made such an exaggerated eye roll it occurred to me that I was rubbing off on him.

"Oh, *you* are no angel." He rolled onto his side facing me. "Never a doubt about that now, was there?"

I couldn't help but smile.

"Can I ask you a question totally off the subject?"

"Please! By all means change the subject." Then he quieted. "Foolish talk makes me crazy."

"Okay, on that television show *Making Contact*, are the people in that studio audience really talking to their dead family members?"

"No." Trinidad smirked as if he'd expected a more difficult question. "It's a ruse."

I was taken aback. I loved that show. "No shit?"

"No *kidding*. And don't think those folks won't get a talking-to one of these days." He glanced at his wristwatch. "In fact, that show's host better look out. He's scheduled to die in a car accident in forty minutes."

"Really?" I rose up on my elbow to see him better, my eyes wide.

"No." He shook his head. "You're gullible. No wonder you believed your husband would take your children away."

I lay back down and snuggled into the blankets. I tried to close my eyes, but meditation would not come. I tried to remember what it was like to be sleepy. I breathed deeply as I fondly recalled being at home, in our apartment, swaddled in the soft white blankets piled high on our bed in winter. I craved to feel what it was like to press the icy soles of my feet against Mara's warm shins as we lay spooned together in the heap of down. I wanted to remember the bit of cold air that would sneak in through spaces in the blankets, made when one of us shifted or stirred. I tried to remember burrowing in closer to compensate for the little draft. I was worried that I would forget all about these things all too soon.

Apparently, I fussed around enough that soon Trinidad sighed, and sat up in his own bed to give me a look.

"Laney, settle down."

"I'm trying to. I'm not tired."

"You're never going to be." We were both quiet for a moment before he said, "Why don't you tell me about Mara."

I admit I was a little surprised. "You already know about her."

"I'd like to hear about her from you."

Chapter 18

Five years, seven months, two days and six hours before I died.

Mara was good enough to get me on payroll at the university. My job didn't pay a lot, but I felt better about myself when I was working. And there was day care which was a good thing. Couldn't work without day care, couldn't pay for day care without work. Ah, the single mother's catch-22. I cleared practically nothing at payday. Thankfully, I liked my job.

I was the first assistant to Professor Mills, a scientist and lifelong environmental activist. I later learned that he had played a fundamental role in shaping Mara's theories on environmental law. He was the driving force behind her decision to quit her mainstream law practice.

The gentle old fellow loved to lecture about environmental evildoers, but didn't care much to write about them. That's where I came in. I took copious notes during his lectures and posted them for study on his classroom website. I was also the residential scribe for his book, which had already been promised to a solid book house. We bonded immediately, and with the extra ghostwriting cash I was making on the side, I finally began to save some real money for my own apartment. I didn't want to get too used to Mara's cushy digs. Or Mara.

She was easy to be with. I never got the impression that she was growing impatient with our presence, which is saying a lot since I wasn't the warmest, most secure person on the planet. But she was okay with that, partly because I suspect she was harboring some ghosts and loneliness of her own. But I didn't bother her about it.

I liked it that unlike the other adults who came into our lives, Mara didn't look upon Bella with goofy, googly eyes, but regarded her instead with curiosity. As aloof as she appeared to be about my daughter's presence, coupled with her initial remark about believing she wouldn't cut it as a parent, I honestly couldn't tell whether Mara liked kids or not.

To her credit, she quickly caught on to that whole baby-guest business, childproofing the outlets and removing anything even remotely dangerous out of Bella's reach. She'd previously had things sitting around that would have given the *Antiques Roadshow* host a hard-on, and I figured her efforts were aimed at guarding those things from being destroyed at the hands of a two-year-old. But when she'd borrowed a crib from the lady in 2C, whose own child had long outgrown it, I thought maybe there was more to Mara than I suspected. It was a very sweet gesture.

I loved the way Mara and I performed our day-to-day operations despite the fact that much like the repelling ends of magnets, we never got close to each other. Like when we worked in the kitchen, we'd simply move around quietly, making dinner or picking up afterward. It was like a polite dance, a mutual kindness and unspoken language of respect. I'd begun to enjoy our comfortable coexistence and I knew I would miss it. Even though our conversations were few, and despite the fact that we barely even looked at each other even when we did speak, there existed in the apartment an underlying buzz of peacefulness and acceptance. Mara intrigued me and I felt entirely safe around her. And that scared me.

Upon rounding out my third week of employment at the university, I went to pick up my daughter at day care only to be met with some surprising news.

"Bella's already gone." And when I stared at the caregiver blankly, she elaborated. "She was sick—didn't you get the message?"

"Sick? Who picked her up?" I felt panic rising inside me.

"The woman who always has lunch with her. Hold on, I've got her faculty card right here."

Stunned, I watched the woman retreat to a nearby file and rifle through the contents. She returned armed with Mara's employment card, fingerprint slide, and picture.

"It's okay, isn't it? She's your emergency contact, so we assumed—I mean, I tried to call you, but you didn't answer."

I yanked my new cell out of my pocket, which had been placed on silence while I was in the classroom. I saw that indeed I had four missed calls.

"How sick is she?" I mumbled nervously. My benefits didn't kick in for ninety days and visions of no-insurance danced in my head. My child never got sick. "What's wrong with her?"

"She was quite warm. There's a flu going around." The caretaker made her best effort at a reassuring smile, but I really wasn't feeling it. "She seemed to be in good hands."

Hazily, I turned to go, but stopped abruptly, suddenly puzzled. I turned back around to the caregiver. "Mara comes here for lunch?"

She nodded. "Every day."

I ran ten blocks back to Mara's place. It was mid-February, and the city had finally realized it was supposed to be winter. The harsh wind blew, scattering snow across the sidewalks and stealing the breath away from anyone who tried to move around in it. I raced up four flights of stairs with seared lungs. I was scared, breathless and frozen when I burst into the apartment.

There was Mara, walking the floor, softly swaying my rosy-cheeked daughter in her arms. Bella was undressed down to her diaper, loosely wrapped in a light blanket, her arms and legs dangling limply in her sleep. My heart clenched at the sight of her holding my feverish baby.

Mara mouthed "Hey" and then gave me the shush sign. I gently tugged my knit scarf and cap off, igniting a chorus of dry wintry static crackles in my achy ears. My lips and nose felt cold. Mara brought the baby to me, but her expression turned worried.

"She looks better than you do. You're frozen clear through," Mara whispered. I only nodded. "She's good for now. Why don't you draw yourself a warm bath?"

My feet practically floated to the bathroom. I undressed, dropping my things on the floor. I heard the door open and close and when I finally emerged from the steaming bath, I saw that Mara had placed a fleece robe and warm pajamas on a small wooden stool near the door.

I was exhausted and my stomach was in knots. My daughter's sickness was added to a handful of taxing days at my new job, and in all it had taken its toll on me. Feeling cold and shaky despite the bath and warm clothes, I slipped into the small room where my daughter was asleep. I stroked her forehead and felt no fever there. I loosely tucked the blanket around her tiny shoulders before plopping onto the edge of the fold-out couch.

Mara entered with two mugs of hot tea and sat down next to me on the tiny sofa. My stomach quivered at her nearness. We sat in the dimly lit room watching the baby sleep.

She looked at me with concern. "Feel better?"

I don't know what it was about those simple, kind words that caused the dam to break, but when it did, I cried for everything—my broken marriage, my homelessness, my job— everything that seemed entirely too stressful at the moment. I also cried with relief that my baby was fine. I cried hard. I felt stupid and weak, but I could not make the tears stop.

Mara set our mugs on the desk. She scooted closer to me with obvious hesitancy and almost reluctantly began to stroke my back. I heard the sharp intake of my breath at her unexpected touch and I didn't move. My fear seemed to ease hers. Warming to her own comforting abilities, she moved closer still and persuaded me to rest against her. She rubbed my back in a gentle, hypnotic motion while I sobbed. Me, the absolute non-crier, crying to Mara, the non-comforter. But she seemed like a safe place to take it all to, and boy did I.

She didn't ask questions; she already seemed to have figured things out. I was slight, and she wasn't much bigger than me, but she felt solid and strong holding me. After my body-wracking sobs had subsided, I realized I was still trembling, and it occurred to me that I didn't feel well. It occurred to her at the same time.

She touched my forehead with her fingertips and her brow furrowed with worry. She whispered, "You're warm. Have you felt bad all day?"

I knew I'd been off-kilter since lunchtime, but I didn't tell her that.

Mara moved slightly and I swiped my wet eyes and started to sit up, but she stopped me.

"No. Stay."

I felt woozy and was comforted by Mara taking charge. I didn't budge when she reached out and snagged a folded cashmere blanket off the desk chair. She proceeded to shake it out and then draped it over both of us. With great care, she tucked it in all around me, and when she leaned back again I nestled my cheek into the crook of her neck. We stayed there staring at the pattern Bella's nightlight made on the ceiling. I laughed softly when I saw that Mara had cut out a picture of a cow from a magazine and thumbtacked it over the painted moon. She knew what I was laughing about and she chuckled too.

The room was quiet and I had a million questions in my brain; complex and heart-wrenching issues that would surely take me someplace I wasn't ready to visit for fear of rejection. It suddenly occurred to me that being rejected by someone I cared for could be heartbreaking. Instead, I switched my focus on my day, but that also quickly came back to Mara.

"Do you have lunch with Bella?"

She answered slowly, as if she'd been busted. "Sometimes I do."

"Sometimes every day?"

"Sometimes." She gave me a little squeeze. "Sleep, now."

"I don't want to make you sick."

"I think you're just exhausted," she whispered before adding, "besides, I'm pretty tough."

I snuggled in as close as I could get. The wispy ends of Mara's hair tickled my cheeks, but I didn't move. She smelled clean, like baby powder. Soothed by her gentle touch, my eyelids grew heavier until I dropped off to a dreamy place where there were no sick babies, brutal ex-husbands or overbearing Catholic mothers.

Chapter 19

Five years, seven months, one day and sixteen hours before I died.
I awoke alone, curled on the sleeper sofa that had never made it to the folded-out stage. The sound of my daughter's little voice came floating up the hallway and I was struck with embarrassment about my clingy behavior the previous night. I decided to get up and try to make amends for my strangeness, but after standing up, it didn't take me long to remember I was sick. I hightailed it to the bathroom, nearly tripping on the hem of the long bathrobe. The little bit I had eaten the day before was long digested, but that didn't stop me from dry-heaving. Disgusting.

There was a knock on the door.

"Hey in there—you okay?"

"Yes," I lied.

There was hesitation before she asked, "You sure?" And

then when I didn't answer, I heard the sound of the doorknob turning. "I'm coming in."

When Mara entered, I was lying on the floor with my cheek pressed against the soothing, cool tiles. I felt no rush to get up, possibly ever again. She gasped slightly and came over to me.

"Come on. Up with you."

Against my wishes, she gently pulled me to my feet and pushed my long bangs behind my ear so I could see as we gingerly made our way into the hallway. With one arm around my waist, Mara led me to her room and helped me into her bed. She pulled the drapes closed and sat on the bed.

"How's Bella?" I asked her weakly.

"She's good. No temperature at all today, unlike you." She cast a worried glance toward the hallway. "I've got to get back to her."

I grimaced. "No. You have to go to work."

She smiled and took another swipe at my wavy bangs, her fingers lingering on my forehead. "It's Saturday."

"Oh." I closed my eyes and nuzzled against her touch. Funny how much I enjoyed it considering that we normally didn't so much as bump into each other.

"When was the last time the flu knocked you down?"

I weakly muttered, "I don't get sick."

"Ah, one of those." She felt my forehead again. "You're very warm."

Mara was gone and back in a moment with two Tylenol. She waited until I'd chased them down with water. I felt sad when she left me, and anxious about the fact that she'd been forced into the job of caretaker of my child for the day. I tried to push it out of my mind. I felt too awful to worry about it.

I tripped in and out of sleep for hours, sometimes waking to my own whimpers. Maybe I was delirious with fever; I don't remember much about it. But I do remember Mara at my bedside on occasion with tea and soup, both of which I barely took. I remember asking to see Bella, but knew it was an impractical request. When my daughter went down for the night, Mara returned to my side, freshly showered and in her pajamas.

"Fever's down." She touched my forehead with the backside

of her hand. "Do you want to try to eat something?"

I shook my head and sat up a little. "Thank you for taking care of Bella all day long."

"She's a good girl." She smiled, whispered, "She's like her mom."

Her words prompted an unexpected shy smile from me. "I'm not that good, trust me."

"Lie back down," she instructed and pulled the blanket up around my shoulders. I relished the feeling even though I knew I should get out of her bed and leave her to the privacy of her own room. But I did not.

She quietly asked, "How old are you, Laney?"

"Thirty-five."

She hiked an eyebrow. "Geesh, I had you pegged for twenty-five, tops. You look young."

"I'm immature, too," I told her and she chuckled. It was my turn. "How old are you?"

"I'm a little ahead of you."

"You're way ahead of me," I said softly, and she knew I was not speaking about years at all. By thirty-four, I figured I should have accomplished something; maybe I'd have a book or two on my résumé. I figured I'd at least be writing for a reasonable newspaper. Instead, I was starting all over again with nothing more than a suitcase of baby clothes and a borrowed crib. "You're a tough act to follow."

"Ah, says you. If you asked others, the reviews would be all over the place. Some not so favorable, I promise." She retrieved the glass of water from the nightstand. I raised up to sip it. "Drink it slowly," she warned.

"Like what?" I handed it back to her and wiped my chapped lips on the backside of my hand. I wondered if I looked as rotten as I felt. I could easily guess the answer. "Tell me what kind of reviews you'd get."

"Well, my parents would tell you I'm terrific." She laughed softly. "Anyway, I can say that all I want—they're both dead, so there's no one to deny or confirm any statements I may make on their behalf." She feigned a swipe of relief across her forehead. "Shew."

"I'll bet they would confirm it." Then I took a breath and went for it. "What would your ex say?"

Mara looked wistful. "She'd say that I have an inability to commit, which is probably about right."

We were quiet for a few moments.

"Tell me the story about the ceiling."

It seemed I'd caught her off guard, but she quickly recovered. "You mean the moon that, until recently, was missing a cow?"

We smiled at each other until she finally grew serious.

"Shel and I had been together for three years. We kept separate places. We said it was because she worked so far across town, but I think we both knew better."

She hesitated and I remained locked into her gaze, my unspoken prompt for her to continue.

"So, Shel was coming up on the big three-nine, and she was ready to have a baby, a project that I wasn't as supportive of as I could have been, I admit."

"What did you do?"

"She started fertility treatments and I guess she was nesting, and she…" She waved a hand to illustrate the painting on the ceiling. "But she never got pregnant. And eventually we broke up."

"I'm sorry."

"She blamed me, as if I'd actually willed her to not have a baby." Mara's voice went soft and she wore a guilty expression. "I wasn't exactly enthusiastic about it."

I considered the woman who'd taken care of my daughter all day long and was good enough to let me sleep in her bed until I recovered. She'd taken good care of us since we'd arrived, actually. Despite my first impression of her in her office, I now couldn't see her as anything but a loving partner and good mom. Try as I may. And believe me, I was desperately trying.

Perhaps she felt smothered by the seriousness in the air. She changed the subject.

"How are you getting along with the professor?"

"He's a pretty good guy." But my look didn't aptly support my words.

"Is something wrong?"

"I'm just struggling with his book, that's all."

Mara's head tipped to one side. "How so?"

"The academics of it all is really choking the story out of… the story." I shook my head as I pondered the problem that had been stirring around in my head. "It seems like he'd get more bites from telling his personal history instead of preaching a series of environmental lessons. I'd rather subtly deliver those stories to a broader audience than to beat a handful of readers over the head with rote information. He'd reach people who normally wouldn't touch a book told strictly from an academic standpoint."

She seemed to consider it. "He's not going for it?"

"He says it's not his job to tell tales, only facts. He also doesn't want to implicate anyone with his spirited recollections. He says he barely escaped the federal government with his life, and that bragging about it would be dangerous and stupid." I blinked back sleep, muttered tiredly, "Is it for real, or is the poor guy paranoid?"

Her answer came slowly. "He's seen a lot in his time. There could be people who don't want to hear anything out of him and would think it worthwhile to shut him up for it." Mara turned pensive. "I remember stories from way back—people would get crazy."

"You seem to know a lot about the professor."

"Yeah, I do." She smiled. "Look, why don't you work up a few chapters and let me take a look at them. Maybe we can shuffle it around and convince him it'd be for the greater good." But when her words didn't appear to alleviate my worry, she smiled. "What else is brewing in that head of yours?"

"What if I can't do the book justice?"

"You will." She smoothed the covers, speaking quietly. "You're shaky right now, but you're going to find an amazing voice inside you. Just wait. You'll be speaking out in no time."

"You make it sound easy."

"Nothing's easy." She smiled as if she was trying to figure me out. "You have good instincts. Learn to trust yourself and what you feel. Meanwhile, what are you doing for yourself?"

"What do you mean?" I tried to sit up, but was struck with

the tiniest bit of vertigo and quickly thought better of it.

"That amazing voice you're finding?—make sure it's saying something for you, too. Not just the professor."

"I write a little for myself. I suppose it's really more like a journal."

"That's fine, as long as you're doing something for you."

I shrugged half-heartedly, blinked the sleep from my eyes. I was in her bed.

"It's a big bed," I mumbled, scooting toward its edge. Perhaps it was the cover of my illness that had made me bolder. "I'm not selfish with the blankets."

"I don't think that would be a good idea," she stammered.

It hurt me a little, and when I opened one eye to gauge her reaction, she clarified her statement. "I don't suppose it would do Bella much good if we were both sick."

I stared at her a few seconds longer before deciding I believed her. Still, it felt funny and lonely. Exhaustion was making me paranoid.

I felt her watching me long after I'd closed my eyes. I heard the click of the lamp on the nightstand as she darkened the room. I didn't want her to leave, but I didn't have any right to ask her to stay. I felt relieved and happy when I heard her ease into the chair in the corner of the room.

It was probably my feverish state, but my dreams that night were a conglomeration of Mara and Bella and cows jumping over ceiling-painted moons and an old, paranoid professor who was convinced that figures lurking in shadows wanted him dead because he knew too much…

Chapter 20

For the second time in less than twenty-four hours, Tatum's shrill scream echoed throughout the compound, this time jarring everyone from sleep at seven a.m. I literally sprang from bed, again appreciating my spryness since my, uh, crossing.

Trinidad and I were down the hall and outside Bella's room within seconds. That was where the latest Tatum-Comes-Undone scene was rapidly unfolding.

"That motherfucking dog! I swear to Christ!" Her seasoned trucker swearing made me sound like a newborn. Tatum was breathless and seething and standing in the middle of the hallway looking more than slightly hung over. She waved the tattered remains of some unidentifiable garment. Suffice to say, McDuff had made a snack of it. Phony accent long forgotten, Tatum made her voice heard good and loud as she loomed over my children. "That motherfucking dog is a menace!"

Late to the party, Mark hurriedly emerged from their suite, tying the sash to his ridiculously expensive silk robe as he scrambled down the hall toward the main event. He put his hands on Tatum's shoulders only to be coldly shrugged off.

"*Don't* even try to soften me up." She sidestepped his second attempt. Both children stood in front of Bella's bedroom door, my daughter's arm draped protectively over her little brother. I assumed the feisty terrier was safely tucked away in the bedroom behind them. Neither made a peep, nor did they show any signs of backing down. "I didn't even want that motherfucking dog— and now he's eaten a thousand dollar Rodarte sweater dress from their spring line that hasn't even premiered yet!"

"Calm down, Tatie." Mark, the friendly neighborhood-wife-killer, didn't seem to be lacking for words of comfort when they were aimed at Bo Peep. "We'll replace it."

"Replace it?" She looked at him with incredulity. "This is a one-of-a-kind gift from the Rodarte sisters themselves! It's not even in production yet!" She snorted loudly. "You can't just waltz into a motherfucking department store and replace it!"

I looked at Trinidad and wrinkled my nose. "She really says motherfucking a lot. Doesn't she have an ounce of creativity in her body?"

Trinidad only rolled his eyes. All joking aside, I'd never used the F-word around my children when I was alive. Seems my postmortem tongue was trying to make up for lost time. Or maybe I just liked to annoy Trinidad. As for Tatum, she didn't possess a modicum of constraint when it came to her language.

My son caught sight of me from across the way and burst into a little grin. He waved at me, causing the raging Bo Peep to stop mid-rant and look in my direction. Of course, she did not see me and looked back at my son as if he'd gone off the deep end.

"What are you looking at for fuck's sake?"

"Ding!" I whispered, pretending to draw a hash mark on an imaginary scoreboard. "One point for slight variation in swears."

Cooper started to tell Tatum exactly what he was looking at, but was quickly quieted when Bella's hand slipped over his pouty little lips. Bella was also focused on me.

"What is it, kid?" Mark, parent of the year by comparison to his wife-elect, knelt before the kids. His expression practically begged the children to choose their words wisely. With diminished patience he asked, "What's wrong?"

They remained stone silent. I gave them both the thumbs-up for their maturity. I turned to Trinidad, whispered, "She's an awful mother. Who upstairs thought this family dynamic was a great idea?"

Trinidad ignored me. Tatum was back on her rampage.

"That dog goes today!"

Cooper began to cough. He plunged his hand into his robe pocket but came up empty. Bella, always responsible, handed him his inhaler and he quickly put it to good use.

"Calm down, Tatum." I couldn't believe Mark was actually taking a stand against Scarlet—and on the children's behalf, no less. Could it be…? "You're gonna send that boy into a full-fledged attack. You want that? 'Cause I for one am really not in the mood for another one of those dramas."

"I. Don't. Give. A. Fuck."

"You let them keep the dog, Tatie, or everyone will know. All our friends were at that party. You want them to know what a hero you are to have not only taken in the kids, but their dog, too."

She seemed to consider this. I didn't know if Mark was really concerned about their reputation or if he was learning to work her over every bit as she'd apparently learned to work him over. It was a psychological hot mess.

"Fine! But that dog sleeps in his cage tonight. And you—" Tatum waved an angry finger at my son—"sleep in your own room from now on. Sleeping with your sister is fucking creepy."

"That's it," I said and started toward them without a clear-cut plan in my dead head. Trinidad grabbed my arm and swung me around like a square dancer. He furrowed his brow and shook his head.

Bella ignored the room comment and stuck with the dog subject. She said matter of factly, "He doesn't have a cage."

"He gets a cage today!"

Cooper was still grinning, staring at me in a near-trance.

Tatum waved her hand in front of his non-blinking eyes. She threw her hands in the air, tossing the beribboned sweater down as she stormed off. "Take that kid to a motherfucking shrink already!"

"Could we arrange a haunting for her?" I harshly whispered to Trinidad. I ignored his annoyed expression. "There are surely some afterlife gangsters we could sic on her, right?"

"Be aware of the example you are setting for your children with your impatience."

I arched an eyebrow. "You think my example is worse than anything that douche-taffy dishes out?" I hastily added, "Now that's a creative swear."

Tatum marched back to her private quarters, leaving a sweater-mess and a sleepy, disturbed family in her wake. Mark sighed loudly as she slammed the door loudly behind her. He turned back to the children.

"You're going to have to watch that dog, do you hear me?"

Bella nodded. Mark got no response from my son and he regarded him as a near-alien. I'm sure he was still processing the fact that he even had a biological son. He also waved his hand in front of Cooper's eyes, still trained on me, and got the same lack of response from him. Mark sighed and started back down the hallway.

"Just go down to breakfast. I'll try to calm your mother."

"She's not our mother."

Bella's self-assured, soft voice halted Mark in his tracks. He waited a moment but didn't turn around, only continued on his mission of wifey-intervention. I was hardly fond of Mark—he *killed* me, but I felt near-pity for him regarding his immediate chore.

"What am I supposed to do?" I wailed to Trinidad as Bella led Cooper downstairs. "How can I possibly leave my kids with these…these blithering morons?"

I followed him downstairs and we hung around the kitchen. The family cook was wide-awake and tearing around the kitchen already, singing as he fired up the commercial grade range. Soon enough good smells were filtering through the air. I asked him the same question again. He didn't respond. We stood near the French doors watching as my robe-clad children romped on the lawn with their frisky, sweater-eating puppy. McDuff was having way too much fun to bother going to the bathroom. He'd probably just drop a little load on the Persian rug around mid-morning. *Que sera sera.*

I noticed with some amazement that there was no remaining evidence that a five-star party had taken place only the day before. The house was spotless, the tent was long gone, and, of course, the lawn was green, lush and without signs of the trample that would normally follow such an event. What an advertisement.

"You know that lawn is ripe with toxins right now and my kids are tromping all over it in fuzzy bunny slippers. Not to mention that dog."

Trinidad's eyes followed the dog. "The dog's not wearing bunny slippers."

"You choose now to make a joke?"

"Kids! Come inside—breakfast!" The good father was dressed in jeans and a chambray shirt that, casual or not, probably set him back a few hundred bucks. The guy was so label conscious, I was surprised he didn't think to have a brand name tattooed on the back of his neck. He grabbed the morning newspaper off the countertop and then poked through the refrigerator for some juice. Both kids came stomping in followed by the dog, who immediately galloped toward us dead folks and began happily leaping and barking. Trinidad made a halting motion with his hand and immediately the dog heeled at our feet, the picture of perfect obedience. It was amazing. Mark was on it anyway. "Put the dog in the garage for now."

"But—" Bella started her protest, but was cut off.

"*Now*, Bella. We'll discuss it later."

The African-American maid came onto the scene and kindly ushered the dopey puppy out of the room. The children reluctantly took their places as the cook began shoveling heaping portions of eggs and sausages onto their plates. Right on schedule, Tatum appeared, perfectly coiffed and dressed. She took her place at the head of the table, of course.

"Black coffee and grapefruit," she snapped.

Cook must have been used to hearing the same order every morning and promptly served her before she even had her napkin on her lap. Mark leaned against the countertop, shook the newspaper out and skimmed the headlines. He sipped coffee. A Dead cook appeared behind him and smiled sweetly.

"Coffee anyone? Fresh pot!" The Dead was much more jovial than the living one—probably because he didn't really have to put up with the mistress of the house. I politely refused, but Trinidad took the coffee and hunted around for sugar. He sniffed the brew and took a long drink, a process that he made look luxuriant when I was fully aware that it tasted like air.

"I'll have a cage delivered for the dog today," the cheerful husband assured her.

"Finally," Tatum huffed.

"Oh…" Cooper sighed and slumped in his seat. His curly hair lopped over one eye. He gave Tatum a wide-eyed look that would melt the average human. But there was nothing average or human about Tatum.

"Oh, quit with the cow eyes already or I'll get you a cage, too."

My patience had vanished with Tatum's phony accent. I snagged a strawberry off a nearby fruit tray and beamed her squarely on the forehead with it, an excellent shot if I do say so myself. Tatum turned to glare at Mark the idiot; Trinidad turned to glare at me.

"What?" Having missed the action, Mark looked genuinely befuddled. Tatum stood up and slammed her coffee mug loudly onto the table. She huffed off leaving Mark asking, "What did I do?"

I looked at Trinidad and mimed a similar defense. He wasn't impressed.

"Example, Ms. Cavallo. Example…"

I heard my companion, but I was too busy watching my giggling audience. I did my best comedic work for the under-eight set. I suddenly grew serious.

"Where do they go during the day?"

As if on cue, a young woman, who appeared to be barely out of her teens, appeared at the table. She was dressed in jeans and a button-down shirt and sweater. Her long, dark hair was pulled back in a simple ponytail and she didn't wear even a drop of makeup.

"Who's that?"

"Lucy." Trinidad looked pleased, downright proud. "She's in charge of the children during the day. She accompanies them to school."

"She's the nanny?"

"There are two, but Lucy is the best."

I studied the girl, who didn't have a curve on her entire body; the girl who, in her boring clothes and loafers and with a dainty Star of David dangling from a nondescript bracelet, was the epitome of conservative-plain. I smirked. "Well, it's safe to say that Mark wasn't in charge of hiring this one."

The kids were happy to see Lucy and the table got a bit noisier for a moment. Mark looked up from his paper. Leave it to Mr. Couth to act as if he'd not even seen the nanny—girls like that didn't register on his radar—and he didn't hesitate to be rude despite her presence. "Pipe down over there. Go get ready for school. The driver will be here shortly."

Lucy motioned for them to quiet down and she calmly led them out of the room like ducklings. Cooper gave me a little wave as he passed.

I started to fall in line with the children, but was stopped by Trinidad.

"Let them go. It's not good to hover. They'll begin to get used to it."

My smile faded. "How long do I have?"

"Not long. And there's plenty to do." Trinidad's low voice dropped even more. "So walk and talk, Laney."

I followed him outside and across the lawn toward the shed.

"What do you want me to talk about?"

He stopped so quickly I almost slammed into the back of him. He spun in place and towered over me, glaring. He made me feel even smaller than I was.

"In life, you did many things wrong—"

I cut him off. "In life, we all do many things wrong."

"We're not talking about everyone else, we're talking about

you. Everything counts, Laney. Everything." He glanced at his watch, and for the first time I noticed it had no standard clock face, and I edged closer for a better look. The screen was a unique hologram, a three-dimensional hourglass timer. The sand was about even, top and bottom. My eyes grew wide as he defensively snapped his arm back down to his side. He continued in his businesslike manner, "There are amends to be made and destinies to be determined."

He started to walk away, but my feet were firmly rooted in place.

"By destinies I'll assume you mean mine. Are you going to grant me time back on this earth if I do whatever it is you want me to do?"

"No," he answered without stopping. I still didn't move.

"Then why should I worry about anything more than just seeing my children while I can?" I had to yell the last line because he was that far ahead of me. "Why should I do anything for you?"

Trinidad stopped, turned around and marched back to where I was standing.

"Frankly, Ms. Cavallo, I don't care what you do with your personal soul, but I have a vested interest in what happens here on this earth. I always have. My relatives suffered for the sins of mankind—some of the same kinds of things you could have prevented, but you chose not to. Now, people are in danger and they don't even know about it yet." He glared at me. "I'd like to keep it that way, so let's go."

I had to jog to keep up with him. Selfishly, I wanted clarification regarding his earlier statement. "What you said— what's the state of my personal soul, Trinidad?"

"That's up to you." He reached the shed, paused, then turned to me. "It feels like you have more to tell me. I suppose you won't rest until you get if off your chest, so please do."

Chapter 21

Five years, six months, twenty-two days and eight hours before I died.

I'd never truly been passionate about any cause that didn't directly concern me. Over the course of working with Professor Hill, I was slowly but surely coming around to the realization that we'd been unnecessarily torturing our environment for years and now it was up to us to make amends and try to reverse past damage to avoid negatively impacting the future of our gentle planet.

Professor Mills was the last of his particular renegade bunch. He'd traversed the globe on a mission to cure what ailed this great rock. He'd pioneered all the classic protest tactics—chaining himself to trees, organizing sit-downs and sit-ins, staging walk-outs and stand-ups—all the while loudly proclaiming before any lens or microphone that would transmit his message about the atrocities of human-caused pollution and waste. He'd been arrested, beaten and personally wronged in every way, a cross that he was willing to bear in the name of saving the earth. The more I knew about Professor Mill's history, the more I was driven to research the causes for which he fought so vigorously.

I would transcribe his lectures then spend a few hours with him in the afternoons, listening and learning. Then I would typically research everything I'd learned from him that day until Mara finally called me to remind me that I was a parent. I'd close up the building and retrieve my daughter.

Nights after Bella was fed, bathed, and in bed, I'd generally immerse myself in further study, poring over books and notes from the day, fighting to stay on top of it all, trying desperately to paint with words an adequate picture of my boss's life. It had to be a masterpiece or I knew he'd never go for it. In fact, I feared that if he didn't go for my biographical-story angle, he'd take me off the project and lob it onto one of the starving interns. Truth is I was only one degree away from that description as it was, or at least I would be once I left Mara's home.

I was saving money like crazy. I never spent anything beyond the few groceries Mara would permit me to buy, and only then so I would feel like I was making some contribution to the household. I tried to make it a point to never rely upon my kind-hearted roommate for anything more than the tremendous courtesy she'd already extended to us by providing us temporary housing. But that's all it was, temporary housing, and I knew it would be wise for me to get that through my thick skull. It would also be wise for me to not always be caught gazing at her when she looked up, lest I should come across lovesick. But I wasn't lovesick. Not really.

Since my bout with the flu and that night we talked in her room, our conversations had increased in frequency, but not necessarily in intimacy. We'd kept it superficial, kept doing our delicate dance designed so that we might never get to know each other any better. I guess that's the way she wanted it, and we both knew Bella and I would soon be gone. In all, we'd gone back to practically avoiding eye contact with each other, notwithstanding the episodes of Mara catching me staring at her.

To combat the extracurricular nonsense floating around my brain, I journaled like a maniac. It was the only place I could document everything from my deepest fears to my silliest romantic notions. I easily filled several pages a day in the name of therapy per Mara's instruction. It worked. I'd outlined two major goals for myself; one—to get Professor Mills' book written, and two—to get a divorce.

I'd enlisted a second-year Joe-College law student to file my divorce paperwork for me along with a standard request for child support, which I figured, if granted, would expedite us getting our own place. It would also hurry along the process of me purging my muddled, silly head of ridiculous notions that seemed to crop up the longer I lived in Mara's apartment.

One week after filing, Joe-College, whom I was paying in pizza and cheap beer, showed up at Professor Mills' office looking like he'd been slapped. The respondent had answered back a firm no to both the child support and the request for an amicable divorce. Instead, Mark had proposed a two-phase mediation; first he wanted to talk with me personally, and anything we couldn't get ironed out, we would take to a legal mediator. Of course he'd named Tim Nelson as his choice to officiate the proceedings. He'd also requested that I not be accompanied by anyone, including legal counsel, to our initial meeting. I wasn't really terribly stunned at his ridiculous request; Mark had to be in control of everything. Sympathetic to my plight, the professor gave me the rest of the afternoon off. I would have protested, but I was exhausted anyway.

Bella went down easily for a nap and I went to the living room, where I settled onto the comfy sofa to better reexamine the document my student legal eagle had provided me.

"You can't do this." Mara's voice woke me up from the nap I'd apparently drifted into. She was standing over me, so fresh from her walk home that I could feel the cold air of the outdoors emanating from her coat. Quickly waking up, I shoved the hair out of my eyes. She held up my legal paperwork and waved it. "Do not go meet this guy."

"It's a two—"

"Two-step phase. I read all about it." She plopped down on the couch next to me and peeled her gloves off. She tossed them onto the coffee table. "It's an intimidation tactic. He's going to make you feel like shit so you'll go back to him."

"But I won't."

"I've seen guys like him before." She whipped her scarf off and threw it down next to the gloves. "He'll make you feel like everything he's done to you is somehow your fault and you'll cave and forgive him and why? Because he can't be wrong. He thinks he owns you."

"Well, I'm going to make it very easy for him to walk away. I don't want anything from the house. The state law requires the noncustodial parent to pay child support, or I would have slipped out even more quietly than that."

My words didn't appear to register with her.

"You'll meet him and he'll say he's changed. Maybe he'll even cry. And you'll go back home with him and in six weeks things will be the same all over again." She looked genuinely shaken. Her voice dropped to barely above a whisper. "And in six months you might be dead."

I didn't really believe that was the case. She could tell what I was thinking, apparently, because she shook her head and actually laughed. "Oh Christ. You're going to tell me that you're too smart for that, aren't you? That it will never happen."

"I am too smart for that."

"Oh really?" She gave a pitying half-chuckle. "But you're going to meet him anyway."

I nodded. "I have to. I called him already. We're meeting tomorrow afternoon."

"You *called* him? From this phone or your phone at work?" Mara was stupefied beyond belief at my perceived carelessness. "Don't you know he can find out where you work and where you live just from that one call? Meet him tomorrow?—Bullshit! He could be at this apartment tonight."

"No, I—" And I intended to tell her that I'd made the call from the law student's cell phone for that very reason, but she leapt ahead of me, figured I was preparing to dish out some lame-brain defense about why "he isn't like that."

"You're blowing your chance at a normal life for you and your kid. You're blowing your opportunity to get away from him once and for all." She sprang off the sofa so quickly she nearly lost her balance. Her eyes were dark, her tone condescending. "And what about Bella? Do you know how bad this stuff screws kids up?"

"Mara, I've got it under control."

"What kind of control? I should have guessed you were like that. I had you pegged as a kept woman from day one. Who was I fooling?"

She marched down the hallway and I flinched when her bedroom door slammed shut. Sometime during her frenzy, I'd unconsciously risen off the couch and followed her to the center of the living room before she'd made her abrupt departure. As I stood there in her chilly wake, I suppose I should have been angry. She had insulted me. But I sensed it was coming from someplace different than just from the need to be a know-it-all. She'd painted a pretty accurate picture of the way my life used to be, and although that wasn't the case anymore, nor did I intend for it to be ever again, I admit I felt shaken that she'd gotten it so close. My confidence in my plan to meet Mark actually wavered. I dismissed that thought in lieu of a different one. How could Mara have possibly conjured up such a spot-on snapshot of my former life?

I heard Bella calling to me from her crib and I went to her. I wondered if my daughter was haunted by the memories of her father's and my violent arguments. She looked slightly unnerved and I quickly picked her up and I kissed her all the way to the kitchen.

We ate dinner alone that night. I didn't even bother to ask Mara if she would join us. Her vanishing act was an effective means of telling me to screw off for the night. Point taken. I cleaned the kitchen and turned out the lights and practically tiptoed down the hallway to give Bella her bath. I emerged from the bathroom and started to put her to bed when I caught a glimpse of a light from down the hallway. My sock feet lightly thudded against the floor as I went to find the source of the light.

I stepped into the living room with my daughter balanced on my hip and saw Mara on the couch wrapped in a blanket. I didn't say a word, only sat down next to her. She took Bella out of my arms and enveloped her in her blanket. She closed her eyes and breathed in deeply, whispered, "I love it when she smells like this."

We were silent for several minutes before I confronted her.

"You laid out a scenario that only someone who's been there would know." I hesitated, gathered my nerve. "Why don't you tell me about your parents?"

Chapter 22

Five years, six months, twenty-two days and three hours before I died.

That same night, with Bella in the care of the woman in 2C, Mara took me on a whirlwind mission whose goal wasn't altogether clear.

We walked for several blocks until we hit Pier 45. The pier, in all its snow-covered glory, jutted into the Hudson and was virtually abandoned on that night thanks to the bitter cold. She led me about a third of the way out and then stopped and leaned against the silver cable railing. Unsure about what we were doing, I faced her and waited. I was also beginning to realize just how cold it truly was. The wind blasting off the water was nothing short of polar icy.

Mara's wispy hair poked out from beneath her knit hat, each gust causing it to entangle in her eyelashes. Under the pier lamps, it was hard to tell if the cold air was stinging her eyes or if she was tearful. It felt like forever before she finally talked to me.

"My father used to beat my mom. She'd take it for a while and then we'd leave. Along about the time I began to feel safe, she'd take the son of a bitch back. He'd beg her, always tell her he'd never touch her again, and like an idiot she always believed him." She hesitated, tried to force a nonchalant smile, but failed. "Then one day, she gave him a speech about being fed up, only this time it was different and he could tell." She hesitated. "I could tell and I was a kid."

"What happened?"

"He accused her of having a boyfriend and they fought. Dad was a cop and he had a service pistol and he shot and killed her. I guess he figured if he couldn't have her nobody else would." She swallowed hard and looked at her shoes. "And when he realized what he'd done, he turned his gun on himself."

"In front of you?" I asked in horror.

She nodded.

I took a step toward her, unsure of my role in her grief or comfort. "My God, how old were you, Mara?"

"Five. That's not much older than Bella." She faltered. "I didn't want to hurt you with those words I said. It's not you I don't trust. It's him. I tried to ask myself if I was projecting my own fears and experiences onto you. I still don't know that I'm not. But, I blamed myself for years for what happened between my parents. I can't stand to see it happen to someone else."

"You were too young to have done anything to stop it. You surely know that."

She shrugged. "My mom waited until it was too late. Maybe she did have a boyfriend, I don't know. But she waited too long."

I didn't quite know what to do with this odd confessional. I wasn't sure why we were standing on Pier 45; wasn't sure if I was allowed to offer comfort and even less sure that I knew how. My role was growing more confusing by the moment.

"Do you understand me?" For all the glance-dodging we'd done for so many weeks, her eyes refused to leave mine now.

"I do understand." The wind caught my neck scarf and

snapped it softly like a flag. I pulled it tightly around me. "Can I ask you what happened to you after that?"

The idea of a small Mara alone in the world was heartbreaking. I felt the sting of tears and I was glad I could blame the cold if pressed for an excuse.

She broke eye contact for a moment and looked out over the water in the black, moonless night. "My mother was an original Riverkeeper. Have you ever heard of them?"

"The movement to crack down on corporations polluting the Hudson, right? Professor Mills talks about it."

Mara nodded, barely smiled.

"My mom and Professor Mills fought side by side to save and restore this very river. It nearly killed the professor when she died. He said it was a complete waste of talent. But most of all, I think he lost his best friend. That's probably why he adopted me."

I tried not to look surprised at learning that Professor Mills had been Mara's guardian.

She shrugged. "And that's probably why I'm protective of the old guy."

"Of course you are. It's natural to protect the ones you love."

"Yes." She averted her eyes for only a second, as if gathering courage. "Laney, I feel very protective of you, too."

I didn't know what to say.

"Am I scaring you?"

"No. Not at all." My words sounded whisper-light. "I care very much for you."

"Good." She smiled, but worry sparkled in her eyes. "So, please understand what I'm saying. My mom was a loving, smart woman, but she couldn't save herself from his manipulation. And in the end when she made up her mind to do the right thing, he made up his mind to not let her. You can't stop people when they set their sights on something devious. I don't want the same thing to happen to you." Her glassy eyes welled and overflowed at last. I moved close enough that our noses practically touched. The time for avoidance and mutely bypassing each other blew away with the bitter night wind.

Her kiss was soft, warm, and ignited warmth in places I

wasn't even sure I had. When it was over, I realized I'd been waiting my entire life to be kissed by Mara Rossi.

We looked dazedly at each other afterward. I was solidly frozen, wasn't even sure I could move, yet the idea of freezing to death with Mara on Pier 45 didn't sound so terrible to me. I suppose dying with someone you love wouldn't be the worst way to go, and my God, I knew I loved her.

She kissed me again, only briefly the second time, and then she impulsively grabbed my gloved hand in hers.

"C'mon."

We ran off the pier and across the street, grateful to the city and its ungodly tall buildings for shelter against the brisk winter wind. We didn't stop until we'd hit the landing outside 2C. Our lips were blue-tinted and our feet were practically numb as we stood there listening for signs of life on the other side of the neighbor's door for what seemed like an eternity. Mara's chin lowered, but her eyes remained focused on me. I sensed her internal struggle; I understood and truly believed her deep sense of responsibility to me and my child.

I felt warm for reasons that had little to do with stepping out of the icy night into the toasty, narrow hallways of the old building. Mara leaned painfully close to me and whispered into my ear the sweetest words I'd ever heard.

"I can't tell how you long I've wished you were my girl."

I smiled, felt my soul light up—almost laughed at my own simultaneous feelings of relief and happiness. I whispered, "I can't tell you how long I've felt like I should be."

Our bundled bodies tried their best to get close despite every garment that stood between us.

Five years, six months, twenty-two days and one hour before I died, after silent standoffs and dodging glances, despite our best efforts to fight nature, Mara Rossi sweetly took my hand and led me up the stairs toward a very baby-free 4E.

Chapter 23

"Did you know that a healthy lawn sustains life? Did you know that a patch of sixty-by-forty-foot lawn produces enough oxygen to oxygenate a family of four?"

Mark's taped public relations approach was just shy of sparkling, I had to admit. I watched him walk along a perfect lawn in jeans and a sports coat, listened to the sound of his twangy accent as it bounced along sincere-sounding dialogue. For a soon-to-be millionaire, his eyes showed only sincerity, not dollar signs, as he delivered his message. That alone was going to make GreenSafe a huge seller.

Trinidad, I'm sure, was making all those same observations. He smirked as he operated the remote for the small television set in the shed. He mocked Mark and narrated over the narrator and surprisingly, my companion's remarks were nothing short of utterly sarcastic. "And did you know that that's only true if the grass is as tall as your head and totally untouched by the chemicals you designed to squeeze the life out of the environment?"

I shot him a look. I knew he was going to unload a tremendous lecture on morality and hypocrisy on me at any minute. He continued to fiddle with the remote, fast-forwarding through Mark's DVD, pausing now and again.

"Don't underestimate the power of a lush lawn. Not only will an aesthetically pleasing lawn bring you joy and increase the value of your property, but consider the life sustainability it can provide."

"Now consider that as a result of your lush, beautiful lawn, you may ultimately need to wear a body suit and a gas mask." Trinidad was developing an imitation of Mark that wasn't half bad. He turned to look at me. "Sound like a place you'd want to live?"

"No."

"Well, of course you didn't want to. You moved." He waved the remote at the player again. "You just left your neighbors to suffer, let alone whatever damage came from the trickle-down effect. Oh, and did I tell you the good news? It's not just for golf courses anymore! A major mass-market retail store already has its order in for this fine product and plans to deep-discount it for the general population. Now nobody has an excuse to not have a GreenSafe Lawn! Sounds good, doesn't it? Someday soon, they'll be burying those Sell-Mart buyers under all those lush green lawns thanks to you."

"Thanks to *me?*" I shook my head. In my living years, it was normally my habit to place my hand over my chest when someone made me angry. It was almost as if the rapidity of my heartbeat helped me determine just how angry I actually was. When I did it now, there was no gentle thud-thudding where my heartbeat should have been, only cool skin and the gentle contour of my ribcage. I admit it alarmed me. I tried to shrug it off. "What was I supposed to do?"

"You were supposed to do something more than nothing." In addition to being dead, Trinidad seemed suddenly to be fairly unbalanced. He flashed me a maniacal grin. "Hey, here's a good one—you know what's more dangerous than those pesticides your husband is producing?" He didn't give me a chance to utter an I-don't-know. "A million-plus do-it-yourselfers saturating every weed in sight with the stuff. That's a good one, no?"

The TV screen lines flickered behind him in a perpetual state of pause while Trinidad lectured me.

"About weeds, did you know that some weeds heal what ails you?"

Again, I didn't interrupt him. There was nothing to say and no use in saying it if there was.

"The dandelion, for example, *taraxacum officinale*, is a source of calcium, potassium and vitamins. Slows cancer and heals anemia. Did you know that?"

I could only shake my head.

"In addition to its therapeutic powers, it is also a food product. You can use it to make tea or even soup. You know who else eats weeds?" Again, he gave me no opportunity to answer. "Cows, goats and sheep. A whole bunch of the kinds of animals you'd probably like your kids to see on their way to adulthood."

"I get what you're saying."

"Let me finish," he insisted. "You know where you get those delicious hamburgers you enjoy? Or why they call it goat cheese and goat milk?" He nodded smugly. "You got it—cows and goats—that's right. So follow me here. Some fool concocts something in his low-rent laboratory and makes it available to a massive audience, who in turn spreads it around yards and playgrounds and golf courses and farms. The animals are eating it and the humans are eating the animals and when it's all said and done, there won't even be any buzzards to swoop down and eat the rotting human carcasses because they've also been feeding on small animals who've been feeding on bugs that live in the landscape your husband destroyed with his tomfoolery."

He sat back, crossed his arms, looked supremely pleased with himself. I'd never heard anyone besides my mother use the word tomfoolery.

"Okay. I get it."

"And for the record—I *hate* golfers!" He bellowed that last statement so loud, I flinched.

There was silence between us. The TV set continued to

flicker, casting blue lines around the blacked-out room. Mark had made a mess of things and I'd helped.

"How can I fix it?"

But he only shook his head.

I heard my voice rising. "If I can't help, why am I here?"

"You tell me."

My eyes flitted toward the ceiling, but I wasn't able to lose my patience like my living self might have. I looked down and around at the burlap sacks of GreenSafe stacked all along the walls. I stammered, "We'll burn the shed down."

He surprised me by making a sound like a game-show buzzer. "Wrong answer, genius. You want to kill off the whole town with the fumes a chemical fire would produce? Including your own children?" He smirked. "I certainly hope you were more logical in your living life. As for this product, there's a lot more where this stuff came from—a production warehouse full of it. This is just comp stuff he keeps on hand to give his buddies."

Suddenly, it struck me. "Wait, if it's in a production warehouse, then the stuff has obviously gone through testing, right? They'll question the ingredients."

"Doubtful. He falsified that information."

My reasoning was picking up steam. "But the scientists will surely know what they're working with."

"Your so-called scientists are minimum-wage workers who hardly read and probably will lose their hands after another five years of working with that high-quality stuff." Trinidad cocked his head to one side almost arrogantly. "Next?"

"We'll tell someone. We'll turn him in."

"You think anyone can hear you? And before you suggest that we have the children tell, ask yourself if you want to embroil them further with their active duty stepmother." He rolled his eyes. "Next?"

"Then we'll write a letter! To the EPA or some fancy-pants senator! To the damned President of the United States!"

Trinidad looked as if I were utterly hopeless. He emitted an exaggerated laugh. He turned and began to rummage through the contents of the same promotional box where he'd found the

DVD. When he turned back toward me, he handed me a pen and a scrap of paper. "Go ahead. Write."

I realized I was staring at him like he'd lost his mind. I took the pen, and using the same box for a desktop, I tried to write. I even scribbled madly. No matter how many times I ran my pen across the paper, no words appeared. The hard ballpoint didn't make so much as an indention in the soft cardboard surface.

"That's right, try all you want, but nothing's coming out." He pointed at me like a real wiseacre. "You're dead."

As if I didn't know it. I furrowed my brow, knew that in my living years I'd be suffering a hell of a migraine long about now.

"What I don't understand is, if this stuff is this horrible, won't Mark be punished when it comes to light that it's slowly killing the people as well as the weeds?"

Trinidad folded his arms across his chest. "At this rate, in eleven years GreenSafe will be loosely connected to a half-dozen cases of cancer. Your husband's company and the patented GreenSafe formula will have been sold to Digi-Tech four years before that."

I felt my eyebrow hike up. Digi-Tech was a huge chemical supplier worldwide.

"It'll take another seven years before testing confirms that the stuff is pure, unadulterated poison, and at least four more years tied up in litigation before they pull it off the shelves. By then Digi-Tech will have made millions and the groundwater damage will be practically irreversible."

"But when they discover it, Mark will still be punished, right?"

"This is bigger than your husband being punished, Laney." He shook his head as if I was missing the big picture once again in our only handful of days together. I wasn't, but I hated the idea of my ex getting away without punishment. "By that time your husband will be a mere twinkle in the GreenSafe eye. It'll be chalked up to prehistoric data and general ignorance. As a result, there'll be some puny fine, which, of course, his estate will pay off in blood money." The phrasing was odd. I shrugged it off and continued listening to Trinidad's speech. "Digi-Tech, with your pal Tim Nelson at the helm by then, will take a major hit. Stocks will plummet. There'll be years of lawsuits, and most of them will get dismissed. Those who win will find that the company has filed for bankruptcy. Their insurance will pay very little compensation. Patients will go untreated. Those who have lost loved ones ultimately won't see a penny in damages. Mr. Nelson will fold under his own conscience and commit suicide."

Figures that Mark would come out on top and that poor, pathetic sap Nelson would be forever ruined for having an ounce of ethics. The whole experience felt like a scene straight out of *A Christmas Carol*. I swallowed hard.

"Think about it, Laney. After all these years, what would make your husband feel like he needed to get you out of the picture?"

I'd heard about the capture and imprisonment, even the deaths of some environmental activists who attempted to take on big corporations in other countries. Professor Mills had explained to me that a different version of corporate silencing happened right here in the United States. It was Professor Mills, opinion that the government had, on occasion, stepped in on behalf of such corporate entities and, utilizing scare tactics, had shut down protestors and whistleblowers. It was becoming abundantly clear that being an effective whistleblower was hard enough when you could be seen and heard. Doing it from beyond the grave would be next to impossible.

Professor Mills had discussed all this with me in great detail for the book we'd finally finished. We'd agonized over the finite details for four long years. Leave it to me to die just weeks before its planned release. He'd guaranteed me that with the book would come a variety of threats to both of us. The preliminary buzz about the book was fantastic, and I had even gotten a little press time myself for the writing, which Professor Mills assured me was well deserved. The book's actual content had been kept under lock and key to protect the professor's identity, but it was already being hailed as the ultimate environmental exposé…

"Trinidad!" I told him, gasping. It hit me all at once. "The book I was working on for the professor! We purposely kept its release to the press ambiguous to ensure that it would make it to print. It was in the newspapers…"

He was nodding as fast as I was talking.

"Could it be…? Could Mark have thought the book I was writing was about his hokey chemistry? My God—he thought I was going to blow the lid off GreenSafe before it ever hit the shelves!"

Chapter 24

Trinidad returned to the kitchen and engaged in conversation with the Dead cook who was delighted to have a captive audience. The odd fellow set about cooking up a storm. For a guy who couldn't taste a thing, Trinidad certainly did a lot of eating. I left him to it. With the children tucked away in school, I set about exploring the modern-age Tara.

I made stops in the children's rooms. As I suspected it would be, Cooper's room appeared entirely untouched. The bed looked crisp and not an item, toy, or piece of furniture was out of place. In our old apartment, my son would generally entertain himself with an army of action figures and his own imagination. It was the latter part of that thought that stopped me in my tracks. I wondered just how many of his "imaginary friends" weren't really imaginary at all. Given its rich history, I could only imagine how many Deads inhabited the antique building that housed our West Village apartment. I very nearly shuddered, comforted only by the fact that every Dead I'd met to this point had been by far kinder than most of the Livings I'd bumped in to.

My next stop was Bella's room which, with a handful of scattered toys lying about, at least showed signs of life. I left it and wandered down the hallway a little farther, bypassing the lavish suite that belonged to the Mistress and Master of the house, until I came to the study.

I took minor inventory of the books stacked neatly in the floor-to-ceiling cases. They were meaty volumes of classics, each exquisitely leather-bound. As far as I could tell, none had so much as a spine crease, which confirmed my suspicion that the collection was strictly for show, probably mass-ordered by some assistant so that the library would appear to have some literary chops.

I seated myself at the throne of the ridiculously oversized desk and toyed with gold-plated fountain pens. I plucked one out of the holder and made big, sweeping strokes across the blotter in an attempt to leave evidence of my presence. Not a drop of my graffiti materialized. I gave up and replaced the pen before turning my attention toward the drawers. The first and only drawer I looked in was ground zero. That is where I found a copy of my will.

It was neatly printed on Tim Nelson's legal stationery and signed by me—almost. I knew I'd never signed a document designating Mark the sole custodian of my children; therefore I wasn't terribly surprised to discover a rubber stamp of my signature in the same drawer. It was self-inking and I stamped it all over the blotter as well; again nothing appeared there.

Being "of sound mind," it appeared that I'd signed the children and their subsequent inheritances over to Mark in the event of my death. My actual will was thin and quite simple in its wording. I had signed the document that named Mara as the guardian of my children upon my death. Mara had also been named the executor of my true will and sole inheritor of any money I might have because I knew she'd plunk it straight into the children's college funds. I wasn't terribly concerned that there would be need for further itemization, as my estate would receive only the allotment the university generally provided to their deceased employees' families, which was modest.

I knew that Mara would be okay financially. She was heavily invested and, as I've mentioned, absolutely brilliant. I'm sure my personal net worth would have increased upon the release of the professor's book, but that was pretty much a nonissue at this point. I didn't see anything in my faked will regarding the book proceeds, further confirming my suspicion that Mark believed that in killing me, he'd effectively killed the project. He was truly as dumb as Mara was brilliant.

Beneath the will was a neatly folded stack of newspapers. I pulled them out and pressed them flat on the desktop to take a look. My death hadn't made headlines, but the *Orlando Sentinel* spelled out the story in a series of small second-page articles.

Inventor's Wife Perishes in Private Plane Crash.

Details Emerge About New York Plane Crash that Killed Local Man's Wife.

GreenSafe Corporation Hires Private Investigators to Find Cause of Crash.

The stories were helpful in filling in a lot of blanks for me. They painted Mark as a grieving young widower and me as his pretty wife who'd met her untimely demise. A fiery-orange picture accompanied one such article. Its grainy newspaper quality was further degraded because it was a nighttime shot, but there was no doubt that it was a spectacular crash. I looked down at my clothing in astonishment and considered myself lucky for having emerged looking as good as I did. Too bad I was dead.

According to the same reporter for all three stories, Mark was en route to ink a multimillion-dollar deal with GreenSafe when his rented plane malfunctioned and he was forced to eject. He claimed that his wife had passed out due to the massive drop in altitude and was therefore unable to be ejected. He was utterly heartbroken, completely and profoundly grief-stricken. I found myself almost smiling at the absurdity of it all. The series went on to say that he regretted that his wife would not be able to enjoy the new home he'd just purchased to celebrate his GreenSafe fortune. He neglected to mention that we'd been separated for years or that I'd been living with my partner who happened to be a woman. How tidy of him.

Stacked neatly along with the newspaper articles was a series of slick, color pages cleanly cut from a magazine. Without even squinting, I read the tiny print near the page numbers to see that it was from *Family Home Journal*, a magazine that specializes in heart-wrenching stories and home decorating—what a combo. The children's bedrooms were pictured in a series of photos, each staged with dolls tea-partying and overstuffed bears on tricycles to look even more outlandish than the rooms did for real. In another shot, a blond, busty nanny in full proper attire was shown selecting the day's clothing choices. It figured that Lucy-the-surfboard-nanny didn't make the cut. Boy, Mark was really setting the stage for his public. I shoved them to the bottom of the stack and put it back where I found it.

It was quite a drawer of discovery for my first time out snooping, and yet there was nothing I could do with the information. I leaned forward onto the desk and closed my eyes for a moment. When I opened them, I could hardly believe what I was looking at. The corner of an insurance document was sticking out from beneath the blotter, insert the if-it-was-a-snake cliché. I pulled it out and studied it. Turns out I was worth a million bucks more than I'd guessed. There were signed copies of the check, but, of course, the original was long gone. That pretty much confirmed my suspicion about how Mark had funded GreenSafe. Talk about a quick turnaround on an investment.

I would have wasted some more time mentally rolling through a series of tired clichés about crime paying after all, but I heard the doorknob turning. I hurriedly shoved the documents back under the blotter and arranged them as they were. I sprang out of the seat so quickly and with so much spryness, I nearly leapt high into the air. I looked for someplace to hide before I stopped to realize that hiding was wholly unnecessary. I settled for backing up to stand against the bookcase. I stood still as the study door swung open.

Tatum had a queenly walk, and if her nose were any higher,

she'd have to have a neck extension. She marched in with her cell phone wedged in the crook of her neck, closed the door and went straight to her desk. There, she opened a bottom drawer that I had not yet investigated and began rifling through files. She made her selection and laid it open face on the desktop before sitting down. She was deeply engrossed in her conversation.

"Four million each, that's correct." She had that familiar smile in her voice again and the accent had also returned, revealing a significant improvement in her mood from that morning. I didn't have to wonder what she was up to for long, because she went into detail quite nicely. "These are precious, precious children, my darling. heaven forbid that anything ever *happens* to them, but they are Mark Andersson's family, after all, and should be insured as such. Don't you think?"

I could barely believe what I was hearing, but I'd already discovered how much part of the rest of his family—specifically *me*—had been worth.

"I already had their medical records sent over. Surely you're not going to tell me that children need a physical to insure." She absently tugged open the top drawer and fished her hand around until she found what she was looking for. She uncapped her little red glass vial and spooned out enough cocaine to give her a little boost. "Preexisting condition my ass—it's just a little cough. Take care of it this afternoon or I'll get someone who can." She sniffed, then rubbed her nose. "There couldn't be a better time. Nothing like a little death in the family to shine some reality on the situation, am I right or am I right?" Her eyes naturally flitted toward the ceiling as she took another quick snort. I was noticing the correlation between her growing impatience and her fading accent. "Of course he authorized the policy change. I'll have his signature on the paperwork by morning. That is, unless you don't trust me. If that's the case then you can get it your damned self."

She drawled out *damned* until it had three syllables, and quickly offset her serious tone with a playful laugh. This woman was a piece of work.

"Very good, darling."

"You won't get away with this," I said aloud, but my words

did not register with her, of course. Oh how I wished they had. "Mark is your problem now," I told her anyway, "and what you do with him is your business. But those are my children you're messing with."

I approached the desk and was standing so very close to her it was impossible to believe she couldn't even sense the vibration of my anger. Any closer and she wouldn't be able to avoid brushing against me. Naturally her eyes never made contact with mine and she took little snorts while speaking into the telephone. The conversation took a hairpin curve and the topic went from the dollar figures she'd casually assigned to my children to an upcoming social event. She was dishing about dresses, of all ridiculous things—specifically what she could get in a jiffy from Vera Wang's collection.

"No, no. I certainly don't want to buy off the rack. It just says you didn't try, really darling." She babbled, laughed and flipped her hair for an audience that she wasn't even aware she had.

I leaned into her face so close that in life I would surely have assaulted her with the angry spit that would have accompanied my harsh words.

"I know what you're doing and I won't let you." I was as aggressive as my deadness would permit me to become. My tone escalated. "So help me God, I won't let you."

Chapter 25

Five years, six months, twenty-one days and six hours before I died.
Tim Nelson had arranged for me to meet with Mark in a
borrowed room at a law firm in Manhattan, not far from the
university. We could have just as easily met in a coffee shop or
other public place as I'd suggested, per Mara's pleas. But Mark
had stolidly refused and insisted on the conference room, a
move I'm positive was designed to make me take notice that
he had friends and legal contacts everywhere, even in my very
neighborhood. I showed up at ten sharp as requested.

Mark was already there, seated in the room designed to host
meetings for at least a dozen. To take a seat across from him, I
had to journey the length of a heavily lacquered conference table
that shone like the top of the Chrysler building. He smiled at
me when I slid into the seat. I didn't even budge a facial muscle.

"Glad you showed," he said in a tone that was two parts

smart-ass and one part dumb-ass. "I didn't think you would."

"Well I did, so let's get down to business." I leaned back in the cushy executive chair, never moving my eyes away from his. And then I launched into the proceedings by going straight for the sentence Mara told me to save for last, lest I should surrender all my bargaining chips. "I want a divorce, I want Bella and you can keep everything else."

This seemed to amuse him. I felt my eyebrow hitch slightly and my lips twitched. I forced myself to resist yelling at him and asking him what was so damned funny. I focused on my props, pulled my borrowed briefcase onto my lap and unsnapped it. I burrowed through the small stack of paperwork Mara had created for me. She had considered that Mark might be unwilling to part with his belongings and had penned five documents and laid them in order for the purpose of negotiating. The one on top asked for everything we jointly owned and custody, which would have ideally started me off with the upper hand. From there, the demands diminished in quantity on the way to the bottom-most document, which asked for nothing, only custody. I'd blown the game before I'd even made it out of the starting gate. I dug for number five.

I extracted the thin file from my case and slid it across the table for his examination. He didn't even look at it. Instead, his face burst into a large grin.

"I'm not interested in your schoolboy paperwork, Laney," he said, smugly assuming my law student-attorney was still handling things on my end. I didn't care what he thought. He leaned forward on his elbows and lowered his voice. "I'm not going to court."

I blinked a few times and then shook my head slightly. "That's fine. Under irreconcilable differences, I can do it alone." I remembered what Mara had taught me about it and tried to sound knowledgeable. "I file and you default and it's all cleared up in a year."

He actually chuckled. "You misunderstand me, Laney. I'm not going to court and I'm not defaulting anything. We're not getting divorced."

I felt the blood drain out of my face, felt lightheaded and

nauseous. My shoulders slumped slightly, but I would not be swayed from my mission. "You don't have any say in it, Mark. I'm filing for the divorce and it's going to happen."

Dizzy with anger, I took my papers back from him and crammed them in my briefcase. I slammed it shut and started to rise. As far as I was concerned, negotiations were entertained and discharged. I'd go about it my own way. Mark reached out and grabbed my wrist. I glared at him, surprised at my repulsion at his touch. My words meant business.

"Let. Go."

"Sit down."

We eyed each other warily until simultaneously he let go and I retook my seat. He cleared his throat slightly and smiled. "Let's try this again and I'll make myself crystal clear." He lowered his chin slightly as if he were talking to a small child. "I was in as big a hurry to sign papers and be done with you, too." His tone got even quieter. "Turns out I'm in a bit of a situation at work."

"Thieving chemicals?" I smartly remarked.

He hesitated and didn't directly respond to my suggestion, which pretty much confirmed it.

"I could end up in court."

"Good luck with that." I started to rise again, but again was stopped by his quick grip. "What do you want from me? I'm certainly not going to be a character witness for you."

"And you're not going to testify against me either." He grinned. "See, Tim here tells me that a wife can't be forced to testify against her own husband in a court of law, and that works for me."

He released my arm and leaned back in his leather chair. He uncrossed his legs and dropped a heavy boot on the tabletop to prove his confidence about the situation.

"I could care less about your courtroom woes. I want a divorce."

"And your testimony is the only thing they'd have. I hear that witnesses are very persuasive to a jury. Otherwise, it's all circumstantial and the jurors turn all skeptical about innocence. For me, that would not be good." He jerked his index finger across his throat in a slicing motion and made a little animated noise to accompany the action. "You can't testify against me."

"I won't. So sign the papers."

He was growing impatient at my perceived ignorance. It seemed pretty cut-and-dried to me: divorce me, be gone. Why was this proving not to be the case?

"You get subpoenaed and you'd have to testify, that's the law. You can't do that so we can't get divorced."

I stood up and tightened the cinch of my coat. "And why the hell should I do you any favors? Have you even considered what you're asking me to do? I could be recording this."

"But you're not. You're not sneaky like that. You're simple. I know you better than you know yourself." He smirked. "The alternative is that I go for full custody of my daughter."

His use of *my* didn't escape me. I couldn't imagine a judge in his right mind giving this idiot custody of a ferret. "Good luck with that."

I turned to go and was halfway to the door when he launched into a monologue.

"The university—that's a pretty nice job, isn't? You've done good for yourself, got yourself a nice little home, set up shop with a nice gal. Her name's Mara. Mara Rossi, right?" He tsked and seemed to savor what he told me next. "I've got some amazing pictures of the two of you together that wouldn't be exactly family, book appropriate, if you know what I mean."

I turned to look at him and he burst into a little laugh. The corners of his eyes wrinkled with delight. "I thought that might get your attention."

"You're bluffing."

"I can have them to you by courier this afternoon if you don't believe me." He shifted in his seat as if to get more comfortable. "You file for a divorce and your judge will get an earful *and* an eyeful. By the time all's said and done, you'll have every other weekend visitation if you're lucky. Supervised at that, I bet. So, I guess you tell me, am I bluffing?"

I swallowed hard.

"Screw you."

"It wouldn't be forever," he went on. "A handful of years

until the statute of limitations runs out."

But I was already leaving.

He chuckled behind me as I stormed out of the conference room and past the puzzled receptionist.

I heard the sound in my head all the way home. I was nauseated by the time I reached 4E and barely made it through the door and to the bathroom before getting sick. Depleted of everything I'd had in my stomach and with a throbbing head, I practically crawled to bed, where I stayed for the rest of the day.

"Laney, are you okay?" I heard anxiety in Mara's voice as I tried my best to shake off the deep sleep I'd fallen into. It had grown dark outside and the only light came from the dim bedside lamp. Mara was sitting over me, stroking my hair away from my eyes. "Sweetie, wake up."

I moved to sit up, momentarily stopped by an indescribable combination of nausea and dizziness. I clenched my eyes shut again and dropped back onto the pillow. I felt Mara's concern peak and quickly offered her assurance.

"I'm fine."

"Hmm," she muttered as she pressed her lips against my forehead. She kissed me there before issuing her verdict. "Not warm."

She wriggled out of her winter coat and carried it down the hallway. She was back moments later with a glass of water. I attempted to sit up again, with more success this time, and let my eyes adjust to the dim light.

Mara slipped out of her shoes and settled on the side of the bed. Her eyes were intense.

"Now, tell me everything."

I gave her a quick rundown of the meeting and then backed up and went into detail about the parts she wanted to hear again. She looked analytical, but not troubled. Troubled was the only thing I felt.

"Pictures of us?" She sounded as if she knew better. "But, of course, he had no pictures on him."

"No."

"That's because they don't exist. Sweetie, last night was the first time we…" She stammered a bit as if she'd gotten lost in the memory of our lovemaking. At last she smiled sweetly and continued on her campaign of reassurance. "The most he could do would be to come up with pictures of us walking to work, and that is certainly innocent enough. Even if he tried his best hand at Photoshop, he would have still brought something to scare you—a message about things to come."

"That makes sense," I said after mulling it over.

"Look, I didn't handle divorces, but I used to see this kind of thing at my old firm. My colleagues dealt with it all the time, and nine times out of ten it was purely an exercise in control and fear."

"And what about everything else I told you?" I shook my head, felt defeated. "I'm not as tricky as Mark is."

"He can't force you to stay in the marriage just because he doesn't want you to testify. He's from the old school—the courts can get around that." She rolled her eyes. "Mark may be tricky, but he's no rocket scientist, and I find it hard to believe his lawyer would even tell him that's a good idea."

"He sounded pretty sure of himself."

"Of course he did. He found himself a few names, made a few assumptions and tried his hand at a bluff. I'd say it's an elaborate scheme to avoid child support. I can't believe what some folks will do to get out of it. Pure selfishness."

"He said something about a statute of limitations."

She didn't answer so quickly on that one. As quick as she always was to reassure me, I figured that statute thing must hold some water.

"I told him I didn't want his stupid money."

"Don't get worked up about it, okay?" She squeezed my shoulder. "Relax, he's got nothing. Trust me. You don't have to have tricks when you've got the truth on your side. That's the way I see it."

I sighed loudly. "All I see is a hell of a struggle and too many legal expenses. Jesus, I just started getting back on my feet. I don't know how I can possibly—"

"Sweetie." Mara reached out and stroked my cheek. Her eyes held nothing but sincerity. "Look, I've got money if you need it."

I felt myself stiffen at the prospect of using anyone else's money for anything. I'd been forced to rely upon Mark for years as it was. In reality, I'd only known Mara a short time, though when I looked at her, it felt like forever. She'd already been too generous with me to this point. "I can't take your money, Mara."

"I'd consider it money well spent. Think it over, okay?" She drew me close and planted a series of small kisses on my forehead, something she did very well and in an entirely maternal fashion. I closed my eyes and enjoyed it. "Don't be afraid to fight this thing. You've got right on your side. And there's lots of folks who'd be interested to know what all kinds of mad science he's been practicing in that sleepy little neighborhood, let me tell you."

"That's probably true. I'll remind him about that the next time we meet."

She shook her head. "I don't want to tell you what to do, but I think the next time you meet should be with your attorney in a legal environment that you've arranged. No more of his back-alley scare tactics. That's baloney."

"Do you know someone who can represent me?"

She chuckled. "Oh boy—I know plenty of someones for both sets of issues—the divorce and his environmental tinkering. He shouldn't get away with that one either."

"I'm not sure how serious it is, though."

She pulled away long enough to look into my eyes. "I remember the look on your face when you came into my office that day. You were right to be scared."

"Oh, the day you were mean to me?" I smiled up at her and she clenched her eyes shut and formed an apologetic grimace.

"Yeah, that day." She scrubbed her hand through my hair. "Listen to me, don't worry about this anymore tonight."

"Okay."

She squeezed me again, whispered, "That's my girl. Get some rest. You'll feel better for it."

It hardly took a reminder for me to know just how awful I

felt. "I don't know what's wrong with me."

"I do. You're a nervous wreck. You can't believe what stress does to the body. You've been down with a bug almost since you came here, but don't worry, that'll get better as you get stronger." More little kisses from Mara and then she stood to go. "I'll feed the kiddo and put her down for the night."

"Okay." Reluctance tugged at my voice, but I felt rotten. "Thank you."

"I'll be back soon."

"Mara." I stopped her from leaving so quickly. She turned around. I felt suddenly incredibly shy. "You've been very good to me."

"Somebody should be." She drummed her fingers softly on the doorframe, looking contemplative. "I'm glad it's me."

"Me too."

She started away again, but stopped a second time.

"Are you still keeping that journal you told me about before?"

I was caught off guard. "Yes."

"Good. I assume you're documenting all this legal stuff, too, right?"

I almost blushed. "Well, it's really more of a personal account of…things."

"It doesn't matter, as long as it's something you can reference for dates and events if it comes to that down the road. You know?"

"Okay."

"Another thing," she said, true worry plaguing her features for the first time since the start of our conversation. "If you're not feeling better by tomorrow, promise me you'll see a doctor."

I nodded weakly, and smiled at the look of pure relief that washed over her features. The last time I'd been to a doctor was for the birth of my daughter. I closed my eyes-believing full and well that I would never see the inside of a doctor's office.

That was just one more thing I was wrong about.

The next morning, with my daughter tucked safely away in day care and Mara in her office, I ambled along Christopher Street looking for the name of the women's clinic on the business card she'd given me. Mara had made me promise faithfully that

I'd go, and had even made the appointment herself. Doctor Zahara was Mara's personal doctor, who'd squeezed me into her jam-packed schedule, which pretty much said I was committed to showing up. I checked the name emblazoned on the glass door with the one on my card. Sighing, I went inside.

Chapter 26

Five years, six months, twenty days and three hours before I died.

I was in the bathroom sitting on the floor when Mara came home. Even through the door I could tell she was anxious to know what I'd learned at the doctor's office that day. I didn't mince words and made the announcement from the safe confines of the bathroom.

"I'm pregnant."

I heard my daughter's voice, but only silence from Mara. I was sure she was wishing she hadn't involved herself in my mess as much as she already had. I began to feel even worse.

"Stay there. I'll be right back."

It wasn't like I was going anywhere anytime soon. My body, as well as my emotions, felt pretty beat up. Mara's voice was soothing as she spoke quietly to Bella, and then I heard the apartment door open and close. Moments later I heard the door again and then Mara joined me in the bathroom. For the umpteenth time in so many days, she helped me off the floor and into her bedroom. We sat down next to each other on the edge of the bed.

My flu had actually been morning sickness, and it would have been better described as anywhere-anytime sickness. I was pretty sure my daily bout with it had subsided for the most part, but my brain was such a wreck I could hardly breathe. I scooted my legs up and dropped my head back onto the pillow. Mara apparently took it as a sign that I was just giving up, and honestly the prospect of doing just that was growing more and more appealing.

"Did you miss your periods?"

"Yes. No." I sounded even more confused than she looked. I rolled my eyes, sighed angrily and started again. "I've had spotting for the last few months. I figured I was nervous. Sometimes I don't even get my stupid period."

"And you're kind of a puny thing, no offense. I get it." She hesitated a second before leaning over and swiping a few waves of hair away from my face. She kissed me on my forehead and smiled sweetly. "Well, I have to say this is a first. I've never gotten anyone pregnant before."

I almost smiled back but I'm not sure it showed. We were both quiet, and when she spoke again Mara didn't barrage me with advice. Instead she only said, "Talk to me."

"I'm ten weeks along. Guess I better make some decisions fast."

She nodded, and without even a hint of judgment she asked, "What are the choices, Laney?"

"I've been thinking about that," I started, gathering strength from her stolid nature. I sat up a bit and tried to put a voice to some of the chaotic conversations that had been taking place in my head for the better part of an afternoon. It came out as mass confusion. "I can't get more deeply entwined with Mark than I already am. I just can't."

"I understand," she said, nodding. "What does that mean?"

"If he knows I'm pregnant, he'll use everything in his artillery—unbalanced hormones, financial fears—*anything* he can think of to get me to go back with him. He's going to be hard to get away from. I'm not sure I can shelter one more person from his personal and legal fallout right now." I felt my eyes well for the first time since hearing the news. Oddly, the only other time I'd cried in years had also been to Mara weeks earlier. She really seemed to bring it out of me. Meanwhile, she probably figured I was a first-class crybaby. "I just can't do it. I'm sorry. He plays too dirty."

Mara scooted up to sit beside me in bed. She plumped the pillows behind us and put an arm around me. We settled in.

"You're strong enough to do whatever you put your mind to. That's a promise."

I sobbed harder and she squeezed my shoulder.

"Shhh…now listen to me." Her voice soothed me as much as her gentle touch. "Let's start by removing all that gray area. The way I see it, your choices are pretty black and white." I quieted and listened intently. She continued in her gentle way. "You could have an abortion, and that may keep Mark from being more involved in your life than he already is, no guarantees. Or, you can have this baby and see the legal process through to the end. If he takes you to court for custody, you turn over everything you know about his crazy bathroom science to any government agency that will listen."

"I don't have any proof."

"Your testimony is credible. That, coupled with whatever trouble he's managed to get himself into at work should get him at least probation and monitored visitation with the children."

"I don't want him around them at all!" Hopelessness resonated in my voice. "Besides, it'll never stick. He's got a lie for everything."

"Then you consider a little publicity lean. You get a good lawyer. Someone who knows all the right EPA buttons to push and he won't be able to get to his car without going through protesters fifteen people deep." I heard her swallow hard before she added, "I know all the right people, but I can't represent you in case I am called to testify for either of you. I'm sure he'd try it, and there could be no room for error."

"Court cases can go on for years. I just got settled—I just

got this job. And I'm tired, I'm really, *really* tired."

"Listen to me, Laney." She shifted slightly to look directly into my eyes. Mara was all business again, the tower of strength that I admired. "Do you want to have this baby or not? Let's answer that question before we go any further. I'll support whatever choice you make."

I only stared at her. It was the same question I'd been asking myself all day long.

"Just answer the question and it's going to make every other decision remarkably easy."

I burst into tears all over again. "I don't want to have Mark's baby!"

"Do you want to have your baby?" She silenced me again with her stare. "Answer me now."

I quieted, and then with more calmness than I'd displayed concerning anything else we'd talked about so far, I answered her honestly. "Yes."

Mara looked genuinely relieved. I had no idea she held any opinion in this highly personal vote, but clearly she had. Her elation concerning my decision couldn't be disguised, and she smiled and pulled me close. I felt her breath catch and her heart pound wildly as she held me.

"That's my girl," she whispered.

But things did not seem as easy to me. I knew my husband and I knew what kind of a fight he'd put up if only for my misery. "I don't want Mark involved. I don't want him to know about the baby."

"Sweetie, he'll know eventually."

"No! He can't know." I felt panic rising again as I considered sharing custody of the children with Mark, never knowing what exactly they were being exposed to. An even worse thought that I could barely stand to consider was losing custody of my children to Mark. I had almost three years' experience that said he couldn't have cared less for anyone other than himself. Having Bella was a different kind of a gift for Mark; she was an incredibly efficient means of keeping better control over me. Now with a new baby, there'd be another pawn in his twisted game. "Please promise me. Please."

"Laney..." Mara sounded exasperated. I knew I was pressing the limits of her legal as well as moral code. "Let's talk about this again when you're rested and calm. Okay?"

"I need you on my side about this," I continued my plea. I'm sure my hormones were raging out of control and I felt so desperate it was actually painful. I sobbed hard into Mara's shirt. What I was asking of her was unfair, I knew that. Still, my fear could not be allayed and I craved her utmost loyalty. "Mark can never, ever know about this baby! Please, promise me that."

Mara only stroked my hair and rocked me softly.

That night after she'd tended to Bella, Mara crawled into bed and lovingly spooned her body around mine. The apartment was warm, which didn't offer explanation for my trembling. The fact that I'd had a world-class bad day might have been the reason. My body felt like it had been clenched up for hours. I nuzzled in as close as I could get to her, as if her serenity could rub off on me. I concentrated on breathing deeply and relaxing muscle by muscle.

I felt myself at last slipping into the place right before sleep when I heard Mara's whispered promise. For years I would wonder if she regretted saying it before it even escaped her lips.

"I trust you know his game better than I do. If we have to keep the baby a secret, then that's what we'll do." She hesitated before solemnly adding, "I'll keep you safe. All of you."

Chapter 27

I found Trinidad the same place I was used to finding him lately, in the kitchen. He was politely listening as the Dead Cook rambled on while toiling with cleanup duties. I entered the room and leaned against one of the countertops Cook was cleaning, and I pretended not to notice that none of his dabbing polish or swiping them away with a soft cloth seemed to alter in the least the human fingerprints on the granite. It didn't seem to bother the man, so I didn't let it bother me. Trinidad, of course, was busy sampling Cook's handiwork in preparation for the nighttime meal.

Cook greeted me in a language I didn't understand, and only then did I realize it wasn't the same fellow I'd seen in the kitchen this morning. I wondered just how many Deads it took to cook for one household. I turned toward my companion.

"It's French," Trinidad informed me. "He wants to know if

you want to try the quiche Lorraine."

My mind was still on Tate's telephone conversation in the study. I looked puzzled, but not about French food, as Trinidad suspected.

"It's like a cake with eggs, cheese and a heavy cream. Normally he would make it with ham, but he was kind enough to omit that for my taste."

I glanced at Cook, who wore a broad grin beneath his tower of a white hat. I shook my head, forced a polite smile. "No, thank you." I turned to Trinidad again. "Could I speak with you for a moment? Outside, please?"

Trinidad translated my regrets and then apparently asked if he could get his portion "to go" because Cook set him up with a plate, cloth napkin and two forks before we left. They exchanged a few more niceties and then Trinidad followed me outside, across the lawn and to the shed. Inside, he perched himself on a sturdy box and dove into Cook's culinary creation. After his first bite, he closed his eyes and chewed slowly. If it wasn't for the fact that I knew darn good and well that he couldn't taste a thing, I would have said he thoroughly savored it.

"We have to step up our game. Tatie just amped up the kids' insurance policies and that can only mean one thing."

He appeared unfazed. I continued in case he didn't understand that time was of the essence, "It means she's planning to off them."

He remained remarkably calm.

I wrung my hands and began to pace the shed. The GreenSafe logo was everywhere I looked. "She must have figured killing me off was such an efficient way to make a buck she's expanding her hit list. How many bodies does she think she can leave in her wake before someone notices?"

I turned to Trinidad, who studied me intently, his fork frozen midair. I was as impatient as I could possibly manage. "Is anything I'm saying registering in your damned dead-head? For my sake, could you at least pretend that you care? You can't imagine how it feels—seeing this happen to your children and not be able to do a goddamn thing about it!"

Trinidad slowly placed the fork on his plate and quietly set it aside. He clasped his hands and studied his fingers before raising his eyes to meet mine again.

"I agree that it feels awful to stand by helplessly watching your children suffer." His voice was laced with overwhelming sadness, and oppression shone in his beautiful golden eyes. It was the first expression of true sadness I'd witnessed from my companion. "You once asked me how I got here."

I stared at him for a few moments, then sat down on the box situated opposite him. I was going to hear the story Trinidad had avoided telling me until now. He took his time with it as he ran his thumb along his smooth upper lip. He looked thoughtful, almost childlike.

"Are you familiar with the Green Revolution?"

"The super seeds...right?" Mention of Green Revolution tickled my brain and I was reminded that I'd first heard tell of it from Mara, of course. But I had only the imagery from her report of the time she'd spent there researching the problem a few years ago. "Seeds designed to feed more people faster."

Trinidad nodded. "Guaranteed to substantially increase food supply to countries like where I came from. We lived in a village on the river between India and Bangladesh."

"You and your family."

"My wife and my daughters, Chira and Prya. I farmed the fields alongside the others, ignoring the fact that the Green Revolution was pummeling our soil to death. To combat the effect and the pests the crops attracted, they gave us stronger and stronger pesticides. But the bugs only became more resistant with each new crop. In the end, we'd only succeeded in bringing new diseases to our land and poisoning our river with chemical runoff. We were forced to search for water elsewhere or our families would starve."

His eyes were sadder than I'd ever seen them. "What did you do?"

"Sometime before my youngest daughter was born, the men of the village began digging tubewells. It seemed like a solid solution and once again the water ran clear. We could at last water our crops and bathe our children. Then when Prya was five years old, she developed ulcers on the palms of her hands and feet, and we knew that our problems were only just beginning." He hesitated as though seeking strength. "She died when she was seven. The doctors could not help her, the same way they could not help my wife, whose body became fraught with tumors. She suffered and I could not help her. She died and then my Chira died. They were all dead."

I needed to ask the obvious question. "Is that how you died?"

His eyes switched to mine, hardened and darkened and I knew the answer before he told me. "I had the poison in my body. I don't know why I did not get sick." He swallowed hard and averted his eyes once again.

"Perhaps God thought you should be healthy to care for your family."

"I believed our past lives dictate our present." He shook his head. "I could only wonder what kind of devil I must have been to be forced to watch my loved ones die all around me. I blamed myself. After I buried the last of my family, I took no more food. I starved myself to my death."

He couldn't have surprised me more. I knew my expression showed that I had many questions, but I could not ask everything I desired to know—things about religion and the afterlife; about punishment and reward. I wanted to know what became of the souls of his daughters and wife; I wanted to know if they also roamed the earth and if he ever bumped into them. So many things and yet I could not possibly put him through anymore pain than he was already in. I could cause no more hurt for the man who'd already suffered so much of it in his lifetime. We sat face-to-face, our knees nearly touching, sharing a parental moment and the memory of his legacy so deeply rooted in pain.

"So, Ms. Cavallo, know what it is you speak of before you accuse me of being callous. Know where people are coming from before you dare to challenge that I have no idea what it is like to see your children suffer. When the world knows that your people are dying all around you and yet does nothing… when your choices are to die of starvation or die from eating diseased food and drinking poison water…" His voice warbled and he appeared to struggle for self-control. His eyes returned to mine and his voice now was gravelly. "Don't tell me about suffering."

We sat in silence for several minutes. Things became clearer to me, like his impatience with my excuses and my helpless behavior. Even Trinidad's near-affection for food seemed to make sense to me. I wondered if it had taken him a long time to trust anything he put in his body despite the fact that his deadness gave him resistance against contamination. He didn't need to taste food to enjoy it; the pure simple act of raising a bite to his lips without worry must have been enjoyment enough.

But I couldn't think about it right now.

I whispered, "Trinidad…my children are in danger."

His eyes softened and his posture shifted slightly.

"But you knew that already, didn't you?"

"Yes."

I nodded, felt more numb than I thought possible. "I see."

"We all bear scars of our past." He raised his purple-banded fingernails for me to see the evidence of his poison. "A reminder of what we've been through can sometimes help us solve the problems of what we face. The decisions we make teach us what we're made of—tell us how we lived, what we cared about, who we loved. But love and the need for self-gratification sometimes blind us to an even greater responsibility."

I felt the meaning of the conversation shift and fault was falling onto my plate once again.

"I am very sorry about your loss, Trinidad. I know you don't think our situations are alike, and to a point I agree. I don't know if I'd be strong enough to suffer the way you or your family did. I swear I was scared and feeling desperate for my family when I made the decisions I did." But my argument was losing luster even to my own ears. I'd always believed that I was on the side of the angels; I prepared myself for a certain amount of criticism my lifestyle and choices might be subject to. But while my lips may have gone through the motions of apologizing or rationalizing for the ways I may have offended the earth or its humans, in my living years my heart truly believed I was right.

I was growing more lucid, and it was clearer than ever that I'd been utterly wrong. It was the strongest realization I'd ever had in my life. How ironic was it that I was dead.

That night Trinidad and I lay in adjacent twin beds, both staring at the ceiling, fully alert despite the fact that it was the middle of the night.

I spoke at last. "I'm formulating my plan and I need to know what the rules are."

"Such as?"

"No human over the age of eight can see or hear me and I can't write even a single letter. But I can touch things, feel things—surely I can make some kind of impact." I rose up on my elbows and looked in his direction. Despite the darkness, I could see him and everything around us with exceptional clarity. I had never harmed a creature in my entire life—not physically or purposefully, anyhow. I carefully worded my inquiry. "I guess the question is what would the repercussions be for any impact I might choose to make?"

Trinidad knew exactly what I meant. "You can bring no harm to living persons. You face immediate expulsion from the program for doing so."

I mouthed the word expulsion and shook my head. We stayed quiet for several minutes, during which time my brain turned out idea upon idea like a movie trailer, each canceling the last out in lieu of a better one. Finally, I spoke. "I need to go to the apartment. Not in a vision—I need to actually be there."

"It's not a good idea."

"Why not?"

He sighed. "You just cited your inability to make a physical impact. Mara wouldn't be able to see or hear you. The flight alone to get you there would take an entire day and you've got limited time. It's not a good idea."

"How much time do I have?"

"Very little," he said. "But you can't be around her in her present condition. There's an emotional toll to take into consideration."

"I don't think I'm going to be able to get too emotional in my condition. I would have been screaming at you long before now if it were possible. Believe me when I say that." I was supremely frustrated. "I can't take your riddles anymore, Trinidad. I don't understand. You warn me about how little time I have, but my impact is limited. I can't make an impact if I can't revisit our apartment—I *have* to go there."

He looked thoughtful. "Do you remember how your mother reacted to your presence in the restaurant?"

I easily recalled my first night "back" when I was in Willow Creek. I nodded.

"The people with whom we had the strongest connections in our lives are always affected by our presence even if they are not aware of it."

Trinidad scooted over and swung his legs over the edge of the bed. He reminded me of *The Thinker* statue. I also sat up and waited for him to collect his words.

"Do you understand what an aura is?"

I mulled it over. "I've heard of it. Colors, right?"

"Energy surrounding an individual. If you are aware that someone is trying to deplete your good energy, you can stop it from happening. If you can't detect that it is happening to you, it becomes dangerous."

"Mara?"

He nodded. "Her energy field is at an all-time low."

"And I'm negative energy?" I was confused. "How can that be? I would never rob her of anything good."

Trinidad reached out and touched my forearm. His general touch was exceedingly cold when I forced myself to notice it. I had neglected to do so before now because my own skin was every bit as frigid. His eyes locked on mine.

"Laney, you aren't negative energy, you're dead energy." He removed his hand and tapped his thumb on his chin as he considered his words. "And Mara has exceptionally keen intuition where you are concerned."

"In life we had a remarkable emotional connection."

"In life you did many things wrong, Laney."

"I know that," I quietly admitted.

"Through your actions you disqualified your own family. You didn't take your marriage vows seriously whatsoever and you made a mockery of what such a union is intended to be." He nodded. "So did your husband. He continues to live his life on credit extended to him that he perceives to be pure luck."

"Will he get his one day? Will he go through this same… process?"

"Doubtful. He'd have to make a very big sacrifice in his lifetime to counterbalance his ongoing extensive list of wrongdoings." He went quiet for a moment. "As for you, you didn't honor, love, trust, or respect the man you married."

"You're right. I did not."

For all the things I'd done throughout my life without an inkling of intelligence, not divorcing Mark was certainly at the top of the list. Now he was in charge of parenting my children, a job he never wanted in the first place with one child, let alone two. And where was Mara? Mara, who'd been both mother and father to our children? She'd been stripped of her entire family inside a single day, much to Mark's delight, I'm sure.

"I don't want to hurt Mara anymore, Trinidad. I truly don't. But I have something that might help her and the children."

"Remember, Laney, that everything you do will have lasting influence on your children and their future and perhaps the future of millions. Make no mistake. Everything counts."

I knew exactly where I'd heard that before.

"I don't know how to do it."

Trinidad was clearly engaged in an internal struggle. He seemed to be able to better convey emotion than I was.

"I have…abilities that you do not," he confessed.

I sat up a little straighter. We remained silently locked in each other's gaze. He reached a hand out, laid it on mine and closed his eyes.

He said at last, "I will help you."

He expelled a deep breath, looked drained and downright skeptical about the decision he'd voiced. "Tell me where they are."

I looked at him quizzically, wondered if he could read—

"Yes," he eclipsed my very thought. He closed his eyes for a moment and then said, "I'll see that she gets them."

Chapter 28

Five years, five months, two days and fourteen hours before I died.
"I have to go away for a while for a research project I committed myself to last summer," Mara told me quietly over dinner one night. "I might be gone for a month, but hopefully not longer than that. I have to go to India."

The announcement shocked me and I set my fork down, its tines wrapped with fettuccini. It seemed like I was eating everything I laid eyes on since my morning sickness had passed, which was good. I couldn't have survived many more weeks into my second trimester puking every single thing I ingested. I was puny-looking, a fact confirmed by Mara's concerned eyes every time I caught her looking at me. She'd made the most of my recovery, cooking up an Italian storm in the kitchen. The smells my early pregnancy had previously discerned as nauseating had been restored to nothing short of heavenly.

Mara's brow was furrowed and I wondered how long she'd been pondering how to deliver this news to me. Bella watched us quietly from her booster seat, gnawing on her toast, as if she also understood the weight of the conversation taking place. I reached across the table and squeezed Mara's hand. I chose not to burden her with how very much Bella and I would miss her.

"What's the political climate like there? Will you be safe?"

She raised her eyes to mine and studied me before forcing a small, worried smile. "I tell you that I'm leaving for nearly a month after you've been so sick—and leaving you with a toddler no less, and you're worried about me?"

"But I'm absolutely fine," I hurriedly promised her before switching the subject back to an international trek that I had known nothing of before that night. I posed my question again. "Will you be safe?"

"Yes. I'll get a ton of shots and stuff." She shook her head. "Months ago, I wanted so much to go. That's changed now. I don't want to leave you."

I didn't want her to go either, but I wasn't of sound mind. In my silly, love-struck, hormonal condition, I missed her when she was a measly ten blocks away at the university giving an evening lecture. I would sometimes leave Bella with the lady in 2C and slip into the back of the auditorium just to hear her speak. Often I had no idea what she was talking about; I only knew that anywhere from fifty to nearly a thousand students at any given time were thoroughly enthralled by her every word, and I felt an overwhelming sense of pride in my girlfriend. Mara is nothing short of absolutely brilliant; stop me if I've mentioned it before.

I brightened for her benefit. "You have to go. It's what you do."

"It's a WHO project—World Health Organization. They selected a team of twenty to go and collect samples and document health cases there."

"You won't be exposed to anything dangerous, will you?"

She smirked, but not out of meanness and it wasn't directed at me. "Those people have already been exposed to everything. The very water tributaries that supply them are killing them."

She looked thoughtful, but turned her attention back to my inquiry. "But WHO takes its own supplies. We'll be fine. They're very careful."

"Okay." I squeezed her hand more tightly until she looked at me again. Worry played over her features and I smiled at her encouragingly. "So, you'll go and then you'll come home and give a bunch of wonderful lectures and write some amazing articles. We'll be fine here."

"Given the circumstances, I don't feel good about going."

The "circumstances" she referred to had nothing to do with my getting over a three-plus-month illness or the fact that I'd be alone with an active two-year-old. No, the circumstances she was referring to was my dismissive behavior toward the entire pregnancy itself.

I think I was mad at my uterus, not so much because Mark was the biological co-creator, but because as a result of my being pregnant, fearful, and hormonal as hell, I'd surrendered everything—including any chance of child support—and had forged an under-the-table settlement agreement. No document, only words and the promise of what was to come should I choose not to follow the verbal contract to the letter. The agreement was that Mark would remain a hands-off parent and that I would remain silent and legally married for five years. I suppose by then Mark figured his old company would lose interest in pressing charges, and without my testimony he'd pegged their case as flimsy, at best.

Mark was a crafty boy. Some—perhaps all—of those factoids contributed toward me having an overwhelmingly aloof attitude toward my uterus and its secret content. That pretty much summed up any romanticism I had about the blessed event, despite the fact that baby number two would be here in a mere five months. This perturbed Mara more than I can describe. Still, her patience with me was unending.

"I promise you we'll be fine. Both of us." And for her benefit I glanced down at my still flat stomach and added, "All of us. Okay?"

She didn't appear as reassured as I would have wished. I got up and walked around the table to stand behind her. I leaned over and tightly hugged her. She set her fork aside, scooted away from the table, turned and pulled me onto her lap. She nuzzled her face into my collarbone and we stayed like that for a while.

"Me too!" Bella shouted. She shoved her blunted toddler fork onto the floor and its clatter caused her to get even more excited. "Me too!"

Laughing, Mara reached over and dragged Bella's chair a bit closer until I could pull her out of her seat and put her in the mix. The three of us engaged in an awkward, wonderful embrace. I couldn't believe how remarkably secure I felt with my newly formed little family.

That night after Bella was asleep, I went to Mara. She was sitting on the bed, engrossed in a WHO handbook about international travel.

"When do you go?"

"Monday."

It was already Thursday. I felt an emotional rush, but held it in and again blamed my godforsaken hormones. I leaned into Mara and hugged her so that she'd not read my expression. She closed her book and dropped it onto the bed, turned and buried her face into my chest as I stood before her.

"Come here," she whispered, and gently tugged me down to her.

We kissed as her fingers worked at untying my robe sash, and when it fell open she wrapped her arms around my bare waist. She kissed a trail downward until she reached just below my breasts toward my stomach, and my body stiffened. Mara drew back slightly and looked at me a question in her eyes.

"Don't...kiss me there. Please."

My repulsion with my pregnancy had me feeling very ashamed of myself. I also felt needy for Mara and I didn't want to share her with anyone, particularly not with a baby I couldn't even describe without using the term "it"–God help me.

Mara felt things very deeply. She was highly confrontational of her own feelings, and for her everything was best dealt with head-on. She had to feel everything; whether that meant she snagged her toes on every rough pebble underfoot or waggled her fingers into the mist of the clouds, she was on a mission to feel every emotion this life presented to her.

My unwillingness to speak about my pregnancy didn't bode well with this formula. Still, she let it work itself out and resisted pushing me to do or feel anything I wasn't ready for. She bore my emotional torture as her own, and that reason alone should have been enough for me to try to make some connection with "it." But at the time I could not; not even for Mara.

She nodded that she understood, though I knew she did not. I wanted to cry. I needed her as close with me as two bodies could possibly get, close enough that I could fool my soul into feeling whole again. I craved her strength.

"Make love to me."

She barely let me finish my whispered words before kissing me, starting gently, softly. Our passion always seemed to advance quickly, as if our bodies were born to love each other. She stroked her thumb over my shoulder blade and hesitated, alternately fascinated and horrified by my post-sickness gauntness. She nudged my robe until it fell in a heap onto the floor behind me, and then with utmost care she pulled me on top of her.

Her touch ignited a quiver in the pit of my stomach. The prospect of not having her next to me in bed each night was rapidly sinking in. Five months earlier I couldn't have imagined what it would be like to fully love and give to another with no inhibitions. Now I could barely stand the thought of being apart from Mara for even a single night. She mistook my trembling for chill and drew the quilt over me. She pulled me close as we began to move together. I whimpered involuntarily at her gentle touch. I gazed into her eyes, feeling only love and silently encouraging her until she was touching me.

Mara was timid with her motions, fearful of hurting me despite my promise to her that she would not. She traced me and entered me only barely. I pushed hard against her, but she looked into my eyes.

"Not yet," she whispered.

Mara kissed a trail down my neck and cupped and gently suckled my swollen breasts. Warmth spread throughout me at lightning speed. She entered my vagina a little more, her gentle touch quickly putting me over the top. I clung to her as she whispered sweet assurances in my ear. I collapsed beside her, tired and fraught with a mixture of sadness and joy. Grateful for the cover of darkness, I felt tears sting my eyes and eventually brim over and spill down my cheeks. I used my hair as a buffer between us and nested it around my face so I could lay against her without her knowing how emotional I'd become.

"You're my girl."

"I am," I whispered.

"I'll be home soon, you know. And I'll call you every day, too. There's a ten-and-a-half-hour time difference." She stroked my back and nuzzled me close. She forced a nonchalant chuckle that wasn't very successful. "Maybe you'll even like having me out of your hair for a little while, huh?"

"No." And then I knew she felt my tears. She held me tighter, kissed the top of my head and cradled me close as I whispered, "No, I won't like it at all."

The following Wednesday evening as I was peeling Bella out of her coat, my phone rang. I double-checked the caller ID and furrowed my forehead, then bypassed all intended greetings with my unique opener: "Why aren't you asleep?"

The sound of her genuine laughter down the line was so welcome to my ears that I laughed too, but quickly turned serious again. "It's four thirty in the morning there. You should be asleep."

"See? That's why you're the mother—because you're so good at it." I heard her smiling. "How are you?"

"I'm missing you," I told her. Bella toddled down the hallway toward her room. I followed quietly behind, the phone to my ear. "It's hard to believe you're so far away. It sounds like you're right next door."

"I wish I were. I can't get a grip on this time change yet. I guess it'll get better."

"Sure it will. How are things over there?"

"A little...dreadful." She sounded exhausted. "We're going into one of the villages tomorrow to have a clinic. They want to get a good cross section to measure the extent of the damage. I've seen so many kids already in this short time. It's hard to believe."

"Will you tell me about it?"

She hesitated, and then said, "When I get home I will." And then she quickly changed the subject. "How's Bella?"

"She's fine. She misses you."

"You're making that up."

"I swear I'm not. The girls at day care said she won't eat lunch without you. They hate you being gone almost as much as I do. Without anything in her belly, she skips her nap and she's a real grouch for the rest of the day."

"No way?" And though Mara sounded worried, I could tell she was trying to stifle her delight at my daughter missing her. "Ah, sweetie, how are you dealing with that?"

I laughed softly. "Are you kidding? She's in bed for me by seven thirty and sleeps solidly all night. I'm the only one coming out ahead on this deal. God bless the day care girls though."

She sounded almost shy as she asked, "How are you feeling?"

"I feel good," I told her. "Mara, please be safe and hurry back."

"I will. Tell Bella I miss her. I miss my girls."

The sound of her quiet voice sent a tingle through me. She made me feel warm, safe, and good from halfway around the world. I didn't want to let her go, but I wanted her to get some sleep, and I loved that I was the last person she'd talk to before drifting off.

"Rest now, okay?"

"I will. Take care of you and the babies—both of them, okay? Promise?" Our connection was so clear I heard her swallow hard. "It's important, sweetie. Everything counts. Please promise me."

"I promise, Mara."

Five years, four months, fifteen days and five hours before I died, I was lying in bed after a long day of chasing first Bella, then the professor, and then Bella again. It was a godsend that my daughter was going to bed so early. As far as I was concerned, sleep was the new black and I was fashionably exhausted all the time.

Mara would be home in a week and I couldn't possibly have been more anxious to see her. She'd been good enough to call daily, often during the middle of the night her time, just to make sure I was getting sleep. She'd also gone to great lengths to make things as easy as possible for me at work, such as having my legal eagle law student double as my assistant whenever possible. He was operating under explicit instructions to get me lunch every day, something healthier than a burger, he'd been told. And for two Fridays, per Mara's specific orders, he'd personally delivered enough daisies to me at the office to fuel dating rumors for months.

I was missing her more than ever, but at the moment that night I was supremely nervous. I had not heard a thing from her in going on thirty hours.

I got up, found Bella's cow cup and filled it with milk. I paced around the apartment listening to traffic four floors below, the refrigerator buzzing, clocks ticking—night sounds. Finally I picked up the phone and dialed the number of her assigned satellite phone. Almost three thirty her time and no one answered. There was no way to leave a voice mail. I hung up and went back to the bedroom.

I wrote for myself for a little while. My journaling habit had me very near the end of book three; they were like volumes in a series. The writing had taken on a life of its own. What was once perfunctory writing for the sake of avoiding bona-fide therapy had segued into the story of me. I spared the pages no pain, but rewarded them with equal amounts of pleasure. I documented Bella's milestones and thoughtfully wove the story of our sweet life with Mara. With reluctance, but out of the promise I'd made to my girlfriend, I included details about Mark and his half-cooked paperless agreement. As my appreciation for the professor grew, I incorporated work tidbits along with a veritable bank of his handed-down wisdoms.

The books were peppered with my favorite poems—some I'd actually penned myself, though I was hardly a poet. On occasion, I would stash a candid snapshot of any one of the three of us between the pages. The books had evolved into a sort of ode to a good life with a wonderful woman and the best kid I could ever hope to have.

I kept the journals hidden away in a large wooden boot box on the floor of the closet. Maybe I was embarrassed about what a goofy read they'd make if Mara ever bothered to flip through one. Moreover, I suspected that I hid them because I'd never been allowed to keep anything for myself during my time with Mark. Mara understood that I required a degree of privacy and she was good with that.

Of course, two weeks without her had me rethinking my stance on privacy. I missed her sorely.

I wrote a few pages and put my journal back in its secret place and flipped on the new bedroom television. Legal Boy Wonder had installed it the week before. It was a thirty-two-inch flat screen in high def, glorious color mounted on the wall over the dresser. I guess Mara thought if she could keep me entertained in bed, I might spend more time relaxing there. It was funny since she had no use for television herself. In fact, it was all quite funny—the lunches, the flowers, and the TV—because Mara wasn't a woman of extravagance. That she was the curator of an apartment showplace full of beautiful and interesting things was only as a result of her extensive travels over the years. It seemed almost accidental that it all worked together, the anti of pompous, the furthest thing from flashy. I loved being surrounded by her things; she was so very much a part of her apartment.

I flipped through the channels and slowed when it came to the news channels. I don't know what I expected to learn there, but I prayed that there would be no bad news starring India or WHO. I clicked slowly through my selections, passing on *Sports Center* and pausing long enough to grimace at the sanctimonious Nancy Grace. I landed on a commercial and waited for it to end, only to discover that the program was a rerun of Donny Deutsch interviewing Ann Coulter.

"Oh Christ," I muttered aloud, upping my game with a few unladylike swears, as a simple scowl would not do. It was in the midst of my mumbling tirade when I felt it.

I leaned forward slightly, laid a hand on my little belly and waited. Two more clean kicks—I could barely believe it. I did a mental math rundown of months and weeks and realized that it was about the right time for movement. Somehow, when I wasn't paying attention, the uterus I was so angry at had turned into a nourishing environment for a baby. My heart quickened as I lay there with my hand atop the smallest bump in the world, and suddenly I realized I wasn't all that angry anymore. Mara would be tickled pink. Maybe I was too.

Chapter 29

Five years, four months, fourteen days and nineteen hours before I died.

I called in sick at the university. It just sounded better than calling in sleepless and worried about my girlfriend. The professor would have to fend for himself that day and get an assistant who was more of a flunky than me to pinch-hit on his note-taking for the website. My decision to stay home threw poor Bella's schedule off even more than it already was, and as a result she actually did eat lunch—with me—and then went down for a nap around three. I took that time to sink into a deep sudsy tub.

I realized I'd fallen asleep when the water had cooled. I'd been out of commission for about forty minutes and chastised myself—if I'd drowned, who would have been there for my poor sleeping kid in the next room? Christ, I was getting airier by the day.

I stood up and nearly lost my balance in the soapy, slippery tub, proving that I was perhaps getting clumsier by the day as well. I wiped off, towel dried the ends of my hair and dressed in a thin T-shirt and pajama pants before going to check on Bella. I stepped across the hallway and saw Mara leaning over the crib, watching my daughter sleep. I gasped.

She turned around and in two long strides she was holding me. She went straight to work doing my favorite thing, planting dozens of kisses on the top of my head. I held onto her as tight as I could. After several minutes Mara gave me the shush sign. She took my hand and led me out of the room toward the bedroom. I waited in the doorway as she began to draw back the covers of the freshly made bed.

"You didn't tell me you weren't feeling well," she sweetly reprimanded me.

"But I feel fine."

"Says you, but the good professor tells me you've been absolutely dragging around the hallways lately. Then, of course, I went to surprise you at the university today and you weren't there." She threw a glance at me from over her shoulder before going back to work, plumping pillows and smoothing sheets. "Called in sick, they said. So I came home to find you and—*oh!*"

She turned around mid-sentence and inhaled sharply. Her eyes were focused on my middle and all thoughts of chastising me went out the door. She'd gotten her first good look at me in more than three weeks. Mesmerized, she moved toward me. "You're showing. Oh my God…"

My T-shirt was extraordinarily thin, the best kind for getting comfy. It also emphasized my emergent belly and at once, I was embarrassed.

"I feel huge."

"No, no." She took my hands and leaned me back slightly without touching my belly. I could tell she wanted to so badly. I saved her the agony and moved her hand to rest upon my bump. She expelled a sharp breath and I felt her relax almost at once. Smiling, she said almost shyly, "You look beautiful."

I loved the way it sounded. I loved the way everything

sounded coming from Mara.

"You missed it last night. He kicked."

"*He?*" Her eyes doubled in size.

"Or she—I don't know. It was Ann Coulter."

Mara was looking at me as if I'd lost my mind. When I explained what happened, we laughed like giddy teenagers. Mara's eyes sparkled.

"Come here."

I stepped into her embrace and she swayed slightly with me as we stood there. I felt her profound relief all the way through me as she whispered, "I mean it—you are beautiful. I want you to feel happy. I want you to feel everything."

She released me and nudged me toward the bed. "But the professor was right. You look sleepy."

She got in after me and helped me get comfortable. I snuggled so close to her we were seriously in danger of becoming one. I felt safe and loved. I don't know how long I basked in that lovely feeling before I fell asleep.

Five years, four months, fourteen days and sixteen hours before I died, I awoke from our impromptu nap lightheaded and crampy. My legs felt warm and wet, and when I drew the covers back I saw blood.

A husky cab driver carried me into the hospital emergency room with Mara leading the way. A nurse instructed him to place me on a nearby gurney, and Mara was already plying the desk clerk with insurance cards and ID as well as details of the evening's events. She was levelheaded to a fault. I heard myself calling for her and she was at my side in a flash as they wheeled me to a little room. There, a short butch nurse wearing lime scrubs gave me the once-over. She checked my vitals without emotion until she drew back the blanket and saw the blood I'd lost. Her eyes went wide with sympathy.

"Let's get you into a gown and we can see what we've got going on here, how does that sound?"

I nodded, feeling light-headed, either at the sight of the

blood or the mere thought of it, I couldn't be sure. Together, the nurse and Mara removed my blood-stained clothing and helped me into an airy open-back gown. I lay back down and curled onto my side.

"I'm going to give you something to calm you a little. On a scale of one to five, five being the worst, can you rate your pain?"

"Two, maybe three."

"Very good." She smiled and patted my arm until she found a vein then started an IV and left us.

Mara pulled a chair close to my side, leaned over, and pressed a dozen tiny kisses into my temple. "I'm here," she whispered.

I closed my eyes and concentrated on taking deep breaths as the sedative did its work. My stomach felt woozy and crampy and I wondered if I would throw up.

"Sweetie, would you like me to call your mother?" she sweetly asked. I shook my head and felt hot tears escape my closed eyes. "Are you sure she wouldn't like to know what's going on?"

"I don't even know what's going on," I whispered. "I didn't even tell her I was pregnant. Just another reason to be disappointed in me."

"No, no, shush." Mara stroked my hair away from my damp cheeks. "She should be proud of what an outstanding mother you are. I know I am."

I looked up at her. The dim overhead light glowed orange around her head and made her look like an angel.

"It's one of your best qualities. It's one of the reasons I fell in love with you."

I realized how clearly my surprise showed on my face. My eyes never left hers as she knelt very close to me. She whispered, "And I do love you."

She'd implied it, showed it in every way possible, but Mara had never actually spoken the words. The sincerity and love in her voice made me so emotional I couldn't speak. Mara snatched a blanket off the foot of the cot and shook it out. She draped it over me and tenderly rubbed my back as I wept.

"It's okay," she said. Somewhat taken aback by my reaction,

she smiled and quietly added in a playful voice, "Don't tell me no one has never told you they loved you before."

I gathered my wits about me and whispered back, "No one I loved back."

"Then I've got lost time to make up for," she teased. Mara smoothed the covers over me. In a maternal move, she kissed my forehead, my nose, and my cheeks, whispering all the while, "I love you. I love you."

We were interrupted by the doctor's entrance. Dr. Zahara was dressed in a black cocktail dress, her hair in an upsweep, having clearly been taken away from a night out. But her expression was one of concern.

"So, tell me about your day," she calmly began.

"Everything was good until I woke up."

Dr. Zahara had begun poking and prodding around my body, and then broke away long enough to skim the patient chart. "Have you been bleeding prior to this?"

I felt confused and tired. Mara picked up the slack.

"She spotted for the first few months during the time she was supposed to have her period." Mara looked at me and nodded. "But there's been nothing since then, has there?"

I shook my head.

The doctor closed the chart and gave us her best reassuring smile. "I paged an ultrasound tech on my way in. We'll get a good look and see what our next move is." She glanced at her watch. "When was the last time you felt any movement?"

"When I was in the bathtub around four." I practically ran right over my own answer. "Is the baby…gone?"

"I won't know anything until we do the ultrasound. I know it's difficult, but try and relax as much as possible."

It wasn't difficult, it was impossible. Historically in my moments of crisis I would withdraw from folks around me, choosing instead to crawl into the deep recesses of my brain, where I was free to worry it all out. But my tendency to hunker down and ride out the squall solo was allayed by Mara's presence. She stayed quietly by my side in the tiny empty room while we waited for the tech to arrive. She stroked my hair and squeezed my hand, a steady calm amidst my internally brewing storm.

My escalating guilt forced me to blurt my confession. "I would never do that to you."

She looked surprised and leaned slightly forward. "Do what to me, sweetie?"

I swallowed hard and forged ahead. "I would never take the baby away from you. I would never do that on purpose. I swear."

Mara didn't need me to explain it—it was the elephant in the room—the unspoken truth that Mara was the only one who was truly excited about the prospect of a baby. For as much as she'd shied away from parenthood when she'd lived with Shel, Mara now quietly displayed every symptom of baby lust, thanks to my pregnancy. I didn't know whether it was the right time or the right girlfriend. I hoped like hell it was both. But all my lovely feelings for Mara aside, we both knew that I had been less than eager to have the baby. In fact, I'd persuaded myself to believe that I'd been tasked with carrying Mara's baby so that my feelings of indifference toward the pregnancy wouldn't lean toward resentment. I could never wish ill will toward anything pertaining to Mara. But now, I felt as if through some part of my own, I'd somehow robbed Mara of her child. Perhaps I'd subconsciously wished the baby away.

"No, no baby," she soothed. "I know you wouldn't—you didn't." She stroked my wet cheeks with both hands, effectively holding me so that I couldn't look away. "This isn't your fault."

"I didn't want the baby."

"Listen to me, you had a life-shaking event and you're suffering little ripples of aftershock now. You didn't want Mark to take the baby away and you were reluctant to form an attachment. But you didn't do anything to the baby. Not anything at all. You're afraid to trust yourself, but I'm not." She smiled, whispered, "I'll just keep telling you how strong you are until you believe it again."

Then an emotion—beyond my suspicion that I'd deprived Mara of the opportunity to be a parent—came over me. It was a sense of unadulterated sadness that I was quickly able to identify as a deeper connection to the baby than I'd thought possible. I felt myself start to cry again. Mara rubbed my back.

"It's okay to be sad or mad about anything you want. Sweetie, those are hard-earned feelings and they belong to you."

The ultrasound technician whizzed in pushing a cart. Her hair was a whirl of multicolored braids, some swinging about, others swept back and held tight by half a dozen pencils she'd hastily jammed into her hairdo. She moved like a graceful whirlwind as she set up shop. She aimed her fleshy pale face and extremely pouty red lips our direction and smiled sweetly. Her eyes were blue pins behind horn-rim glasses and her bangs were iron-crimped blond, obviously bleached as evidenced by the two inches of dark roots she had working up top. She extended a pudgy hand and quietly introduced herself.

"I'm Valentine, the ultrasound gal. Glad to meet you."

Mara, who appeared to be taking inventory of the colorful young woman's appearance, had quickly concluded that she was okay, only quirky, and met her handshake with enthusiasm. Valentine then clapped her hands together. I rolled from my side onto my back. The tech plugged a pair of earbuds into her ears. With utmost care she moved my gown to expose my belly and wielded a bottle of gel above me. She paused, eyes clenched shut, bottle clamped in her grip high above me.

At last, Mara spoke. "Are you praying?"

Valentine broke her trance and smiled. "Oh no—I'm trying to warm the gel bottle before I give it a squirt." She waved the bottle over the machine in reference. "All this new-fangled technology and they haven't figured out how to properly warm this freezing gel? Sounds like a man's invention to me." She smiled, shrugged and then with apology and a little grimace, squeezed a few ounces of gel onto my stomach. She was absolutely right about it being icy cold. Valentine poised the ultrasound wand over my belly and went to work rolling it around, pausing now and again.

The room was silent save for the soft buzz of the equipment. As the monitor was facing away from us, we could only watch Valentine's rather animated face for any sign as to what she was seeing.

"Ah—here we go." She yanked one earbud out and turned the monitor toward us. "There's our little guy."

I could barely believe it. A squirmy paisley-looking image

was on her screen in full, living color!

"The baby's okay?" I craned to see better, ashamed of myself for my refusal to watch the first-offered ultrasound weeks earlier. I'd kindly offered that I wanted to wait for Mara to be in town so that we could see the baby for the first time, together. Perhaps I was still in avoidance. Now, I was amazed to see so much action taking place inside my still relatively small belly. "It's fine?"

"Looks like it to me. Kid's a wiggle worm, I'll tell you that much." She blew her wrinkled bangs out of her eyes and made a low funny sound. "You're gonna have your hands full with this one, mamas. Oh boy."

My laughter sounded in response to my pure relief. I looked at Mara, who was still utterly mesmerized at what was taking place on the monitor.

"You said little guy—can you tell that the baby's a boy?"

Valentine unwound one of the many pencils she had jammed in that wild, hairy head of hers. She used it as a pointer on the screen. "It's hard to say at this stage, but see that there?" I didn't, but I nodded. "My vote's for blue."

"You're kidding?" I leaned up and squinted to see better, but Mara's hand protectively guarded me from rising up any farther.

"Can you move that monitor closer so she can get a better look?" Mara was still in business mode, and Valentine was certainly obliging. "What about the blood? There was…a lot."

Valentine shrugged her round shoulders and pursed her cherry lips. "It's hard to say. A lot of things happen during pregnancy that are still considered within normal parameters." She pressed random buttons and the machine purred loudly. "Doc will be back in to tell you more. I'm just the photographer."

With that, she began to collect the images that were spitting out of the machine.

"And a darn good one, if I do say so myself." She handed Mara a half dozen small full color images of the baby. Valentine's grin stretched ear to ear. "Baby's first picture and I got to take it. I am one lucky gal."

We thanked her as she packed up her equipment and scooted the works out of the room.

Mara was awestruck. I tried to sit up again and this time she did not stop me. Instead, she leaned closer and enveloped me in her arms, still clutching the pictures.

At three a.m. I awoke with a start in a silent apartment. The moon was bright and round and cast varying hues of blue all over the bedroom. I was alone. I drew back the covers and padded down the hallway following a different kind of light until I found Mara. She was hunched over the computer keyboard in the newly improvised office, which was actually a corner of the dining room. The buzzing was the printer, and when it finished printing she stacked the papers together neatly and set them aside. I softly cleared my throat and she whirled around.

"Are you okay?" She was out of her seat and across the room in a split second. I nodded and smiled at her. She wore pajama pants and a sweatshirt with her girl genius glasses perched atop her nose. She hurriedly removed them and pulled me to her. "You shouldn't be out of bed."

"Dr. Zahara didn't tell me to stay in bed. In fact, she said exercise was good for me."

"But you just went to bed two hours ago." She rubbed my back and I responded by nestling my cheek into her shoulder. I closed my eyes and enjoyed being so close to her. "I woke up and you were gone. What are you doing out here?"

"Nothing, just a little research, that's all." She waved her hand at the mess dismissively. "It can wait. Let's get you back to bed."

I gently broke away from her and wandered over to the corner of the room. The desk, chair, and floor all around the computer were littered with dozens of pages of what looked like a bunch of scientific mumbo-jumbo. I stooped down and picked up a single page and gave it the once-over. I looked at Mara.

"What is this?"

She rolled her eyes, clearly angry that she'd even approached making me nervous.

"It's nothing, honestly."

I began to read aloud. "Birth defects, Parkinson's disease, miscarriage, cancers, fetal death, childhood asthma, neuroblastoma…" I shook my head. "What kind of thing causes all this?"

She paused a beat. "Pesticides."

"I see," I practically whispered and handed the page back. She took it and dropped it. I watched it feather to the floor as she pulled me close. She rocked me gently as we stood together in the middle of the dining room.

"I just want you to be safe, that's all," she whispered. "And I want you to be in bed."

"I can't sleep very well when you're not there," I told her.

She killed the lights and steered me down the hallway toward the bedroom. "Do you feel okay?"

"Yes."

"No cramps or bleeding?"

I shook my head. She drew back the covers and waited for me to climb into bed before she did.

She said, "I just had a little freak-out, I guess. I'm sorry. I'm a research maniac, nature of the job."

"Do you think Mark's chemicals will cause problems?"

"It's hard to say. Probably not. I just don't want to overlook anything." She was quiet for a second. "Do me a favor and promise me you won't read any of that stuff. I'll throw it out, okay?"

"Okay, I promise."

I thought she'd fallen asleep and it startled me when after several long minutes she spoke again. "I think about the stuff my girls were exposed to and it scares the hell out of me. And then I think about Mark hitting you—ever, and I want to kill him. I just don't know what kind of person could hurt you, Laney. I just don't."

Mara cried silently, this I knew because I could feel the soft heave of her body spooned around mine. I turned around to face her and snuggled in tight. I kissed her wet eyes, her nose, her cheeks and more, all the while whispering, "I love you. I love you."

Chapter 30

Five years, one month, twenty-two days and six hours before I died.
June in New York was mild, giving its residents the sinking feeling that the city was holding out to hit them with a scorching July and August. By then, I was performing the bulk of my university duties from my home even though my due date wasn't until September. Just a little on the paranoid side, Mara and the professor had set me up pretty good at home. A student assistant live-streamed the lectures right to my computer where I took notes and posted summaries on the classroom website. I even worked on Professor Mills' book at home. Basically, I only journeyed into the university to get a little sunshine and exercise and to avoid feeling altogether useless. Same as when I was carrying Bella, I wasn't really big with this baby either. All the same, it didn't stop me from feeling bulky and awkward.

On a late Friday afternoon, I went on one of these treks

and took Bella along with me. On the way back she fell asleep in her stroller, and when we reached the building I abandoned the thing at the door and carried her up four exhausting flights of stairs to the apartment. I was eager to lay her down for a nap, but was caught off guard by the sound of women talking and laughing down the hallway of the apartment. I followed the noise until I reached Bella's room. I pushed the door open and stopped in my tracks.

A woman with a sharp copper and blond-streaked bob was balanced atop an exceptionally tall ladder. She had a paintbrush in hand, poised toward the ceiling, and a bottle of beer teetered on the top rung. I recognized Shel's face from a picture I'd come across chucked in a drawer when I was cleaning up one afternoon months earlier. The picture had failed to reveal that she was beautiful and slim and that wearing short-shorts, her legs looked like they went on forever.

Mara sat on the floor keeping her company, also sipping a beer. They were thoroughly engrossed in conversation when they saw me at the same time. I can't say what I was thinking, but I backed out of the room and headed for the apartment door. Mara was up and lightly jogged down the hall after me. When she reached us she planted a kiss on my forehead and then one on Bella's sleepy head. She smiled and kindly asked where I was going.

"I was…just going out for tea."

Mara's eyes flickered with a fair amount of amusement, but she didn't laugh. Instead, she took Bella out of my arms and opened the apartment door. "Come on. I'll go with you."

With Bella back in the stroller, we pushed her along the sidewalk for the block it took us to get to The Bean Cup on Charles Street. Mara ordered us two decaffeinated hot chai teas and we sat nearly alone in the small lobby. The owners were moving about the kitchen area preparing to close, but they knew us well by then and insisted we take our time. The baby slept in the stroller and there was nothing to distract us from our few strange moments. Mara finally addressed the subject of the not-so-stranger in the baby's room.

"That was Shel. I guess you probably figured that out. I asked her to paint an actual cow over the moon since the paper one kept falling down. I mean, she started the painting so I thought it was appropriate that she finish it for the sake of continuity. She admitted she'd never had a cow in her initial art vision." She hooked air quotes and chuckled, but turned serious. "I hope you don't mind."

"I don't mind."

"Sweetie…" She smiled and patted my arm, whispered, "It kind of seems like you mind. You know I would never try to do anything to hurt you, don't you?"

I'd heard those words before, countless times out of Mark, but I knew it was different with Mara. In my heart I knew she was a solid figure, true to the core.

"I do know that." I answered quietly, and I truly did. The shop owner's son emerged from the back room and hurriedly swished a mop around the tiled floor. He nodded and smiled and then ducked out of sight again. I felt overcome with embarrassment and other emotions. "I'm sorry. I don't know what's wrong with me."

Mara reached across the small table and squeezed my hand. "I should have asked you if it would bother you. Or, at least I could have warned you about what I was doing, huh?"

"No, don't be silly." I felt a sob building, but repressed it with all my might. I flipped my hand over and squeezed hers right back. "It's your place. You don't have to ask me anything."

She released her hold and scrubbed her hands through her hair, tousling it thoroughly. Her eyes turned dark, nervousness emanated from her and I felt a declaration of sorts coming on. I swallowed hard and braced myself for whatever was to come, but nothing about it felt bad.

"Every time we come to this café I think about meeting you here that day," she said, smiling.

So did I; I was fresh out of Mark's house and with a baby, alone in the city.

"I was pretty scared." I made a nervous little laugh before turning serious. "You rescued me."

Mara wasn't in the habit of becoming tongue-tied—she would either say something or she wouldn't. But her expression at the moment looked as though putting her thoughts into words would be performed with the same ease one reserved for eating shards of glass. She took a deep breath. "You also rescued me."

I stared at her. "How do you figure?"

"I didn't trust people. I had my work and I wasn't looking for anything or anyone." She hesitated. "I don't want to think of the apartment as my place or my things. You see, I don't want to think of Bella as your daughter or the baby as your baby." She shook her head, mumbled, "Boy, this is really tough for me."

"I know," I gently encouraged her. "Go on, please."

"Sweetie, I want ours." Her voice was a raspy whisper. "I want to share all those things with you—I want *ours*."

I didn't know what to say.

"I love you all very much. Stay with me."

My shoulders slumped slightly at the soft look in her eye. "Of course we will."

"I mean for good."

She scooted her chair back so that she could face me directly. Mara leaned her forehead against mine, but held back enough to see my expression. She laid her fist in my hand, and when she unclenched her fingers a simple platinum band was lying in my upturned palm. I was stunned.

"I know you're technically already married, but I wondered if you could pretend that it's to me."

I remained staring at it. I'd previously never been attracted to the idea of marriage, particularly not my own. And legally I was married. And I suppose legally I couldn't marry my girlfriend. Those were the reasons that dictated I could not marry the only person I would ever love enough to be with for as long as we both shall live. Overcome with these notions and the contrast of pure joy, I began to cry.

Mara looked mildly confused, and with some hesitation drew me close and I cried into her collar for all I was worth. At last I pulled back, struggling to compose myself. Mara's eyes asked me the question again and this time I nodded. She took the ring from my hand and placed it on my finger. I threw my arms around her and held her tight right there in the coffee shop.

"I love you very much," she whispered in my ear as we clung to each other.

"I love you right back." I told her. "I do, I do, I do…"

Shel had gathered her painting tools together and was almost out the door when we arrived home. I stopped her before she made her exit while Mara took Bella to the living room and eased into the rocker.

"I guess you've figured out that I'm Laney." I held out my hand, feeling embarrassed. "I'm sorry, I'm ashamed of my behavior a while ago."

Shel bypassed my intended handshake and pulled me into a hug. When she released me, she was smiling.

"Hormones," she said. "Blame it on them for as long as you possibly can. I know I did."

"I didn't know you had a child."

"My partner Terri and I have two children. Of course, one of them is a Labradoodle." She laughed quietly, shooting my sleeping daughter a glance. "Elizabeth is really about the best thing that's ever happened to us, but you already know that because you've got Bella."

I nodded. Shel watched Mara in the rocking chair and we listened to her raspy voice sing a song barely audible from where we stood.

"You know, I think I was wrong. I guess Mara is parenting material after all."

I smiled, whispered more to me than to her, "I think she really is."

I saw Shel out and locked the door before crossing the floor to where my family was. I perched myself on the ottoman across from them. Mara looked at me, her eyes dancing, and her heart so full of love I could feel it from there.

Chapter 31

Lucy, the nanny, paraded the children into Bella's bedroom, but all order went out the door when they found me waiting for them there. My children ambushed me with the same after-school vigor as they had in life. I held them tightly for several seconds and listened as Cooper chattered about his day in preschool. Lucy interrupted them momentarily and I motioned for the children to be silent and mindful of the nanny for fear that we would give away our "secret."

"Cooper, it's time for your afternoon dose." Lucy held out Cooper's inhaler. He reluctantly dragged himself away from me and went to her, obediently accepted his inhaler. He took a puff and then handed it back to the nanny. She promptly dropped it into the pocket of her oversized smock and then made a notation in a little spiral-bound journal. "Always remember, when you wake up and when you get home from school. Good boy."

I cannot describe the relief I felt knowing this young woman was in charge of my son's medication. He required two daily metered doses that Mara had been in charge of dispensing. There was also a standby emergency inhaler. It was a strict regimen that took a little getting used to, and frankly I'm not sure Tatum knew anything about medication beyond what she could administer through her nose.

I remained silent as Lucy headed for the door. She turned to quietly address the room before making her departure. Everything about her was downright nerdy and highly reliable.

"I'm going to get some tea. Change your clothes and I'll be back up in a little while to read you a chapter of *Knights of the Roundtable*."

Cooper bounded over to her and happily kissed the young woman's hand.

"Bye m'lady!"

Their sweet interaction surprised me. No wonder Trinidad was fond of Lucy; she had a very nice way with children.

She patted him on the head and smiled. "Very nice, thank you." Her voice was whisper soft when she added, "And keep it down, please, or the mistress of the house will come speak with you about it."

They eagerly nodded and as soon as she was gone, Cooper came right over to me.

"Let's go get McDuff!"

Bella put her hands on both his small shoulders and steered him toward the bed like a little mother. "First things first—change clothes."

I wanted to go to my little boy, unbutton his uniform shirt and tug it over his curly head, but Bella had moved in and was assisting him, and again I reminded myself I wouldn't be around to help much longer. I wondered if I'd get to see them again—if I'd get to see anyone again, for that matter. It was alarming to me how little they actually needed me.

We were interrupted by Trinidad's entrance. He gave the kids a curt wave and turned his attention to me. "I need to speak with you."

I followed my companion into the hallway. He talked as fast

as he walked.

"They've been called to an emergency hearing."

"Hearing?" I was trying to catch up.

"Yes." He didn't elaborate, only raised his arm and gave his wristwatch a look. There was very little sand left in the hourglass. I swallowed hard.

We silently passed Lucy on the service stairwell. She moved gracefully, her back straight, delicately balancing her china cup of tea on its saucer. I was suffering a unique case of human envy that the nanny would be spending the afternoon with my children. Clearly I was not going to get any more information from Trinidad at the moment. I sighed and blindly followed him.

In the lobby of the Orange County Courthouse, we breezed through security unnoticed, hot on the heels of Tatum Mark and Attorney Nelson. They were clearly frustrated and as soon as we entered the assigned courtroom I discovered that they had very good reason to be.

"All rise!" the bailiff announced immediately upon entry of the goon squad. A woman stood poised at a podium situated before the judge in the intimate courtroom setting. When she turned to see the new entrants, I gasped. It was Mara Rossi.

She looked absolutely beautiful wearing an impeccable tweed jacket and—gulp—a skirt. My sweet Mara was looking as though she'd pioneered the concept of confidence. She regarded Tatum and Mark only with brief eye contact and waited for the judge to call proceedings to order. Trinidad took a seat in the back area of the courtroom, and from the corner of my eye I saw him pat the bench for me to join him. I ignored him and wandered toward the front, opting for a better view very near the judge's bench, but far enough away from Mara to avoid tainting her with dead energy. I had to get a better look at her.

"Let the record show that Judge Timmons—that's me—waits for *no one*. Is that clear, Mr. Andersson?" The judge was a grandfatherly African-American gentleman who wore thick glasses and a look of pure disdain for the newly assembled. His voice was as deep and powerful sounding as Samuel L. Jackson's. Just as intimidating, too. "Everyone? Do I make myself clear?"

Nelson cleared his throat and offered a little smile. "Our apologies Your Honor—we only just got word of—"

"Am I *clear?*" Judge Timmons also clearly didn't wait for excuses.

"Very clear," mumbled Nelson.

"Good. Now everybody take a seat and using as little extracurricular language as possible, somebody tell me why we're assembled at an emergency hearing…" He raised his arm and squinted at his oversized watch, sighed and added, "*Long after I'm supposed to be home having my supper?*"

Mara stood. "Your Honor, may I begin?"

"You may."

"I wish to file an injunction for immediate removal of Bella and Cooper Cavallo-Andersson from the residence of Mark Andersson. I also wish to file a subsequent temporary restraining order against Mr. Andersson on behalf of the minor children until this issue is resolved and permanent custody is decided by the court. I request that the children are immediately relocated to New York to begin exploring custody options in that state—"

"Hold up—on what grounds for any of this?" Nelson nearly cut her off.

Mara didn't let his rudeness faze her and remained looking at Judge Timmons.

"Racketeering."

"Are you the children's attorney, Ms. Rossi?" The judge was momentarily confused.

"She's their dead mother's *lover*, Your Honor!" It was Nelson.

"I am acting as the children's advocate, as I cannot be appointed or employed to represent them on this matter."

"Nor will you ever be appointed or employed!" Nelson laughed, beads of sweat forming on his forehead. He looked incredulous. "Your Honor—this is a ridiculous waste of everyone's time. The Andersson children have a perfectly good home with responsible individuals all around them who care for them. The parents weren't even divorced at the time of Ms.

Cavallo's death, and there is no reason the children shouldn't reside with her husband. This is a moot point." He looked directly at Mara. "Ms. Rossi is a sore loser, nothing more."

The judge was also growing impatient. "On what grounds do you allege racketeering Ms. Rossi? And given the circumstances the opposing counsel laid out, this had better be good."

"I have an affidavit supporting extortion, terrorism and possession of a controlled substance." She raised the folder for demonstrative purposes.

Nelson shrugged. "We don't have copies of any of that information."

"I also have record of a previously filed injunction as well as an independent investigator's report of the plane crash that took Ms. Cavallo's life—a plane piloted by her estranged husband who walked away unharmed."

"Absurd! Terrorism and extortion? None of that will stick!" Nelson was sweating up a storm.

"Don't forget about possession of a controlled substance," she finished big before looking squarely at the opposing counsel. Without even flinching, she added, "And that will stick."

"Controlled substance?" Nelson raised his voice several notches. He looked at the judge, his mood turning smug. "Your Honor, I will be filing charges on behalf of Mark Andersson alleging slander by Ms. Rossi. She has tried to damage his good name here this evening."

Judge Timmons remained stolid. He looked at his bailiff. "Get me that stuff, would you, Robert?"

The lanky younger man approached Mara and she presented him the legal collection she'd referenced. The judge squinted through his glasses as he looked over the information. "This independent investigator was hired by you, Ms. Rossi, and not the one from the FAA, correct?"

"That's correct Your Honor. There is no finalized FAA report as of yet."

"Ridiculous," Nelson spat.

"Counselor, if you cannot refrain from belittling Ms. Rossi, I'll allow her to counterfile a complaint of slander." He issued the warning without looking up from his paperwork. "Or maybe

I'll just cite you for contempt for being arrogant. How would that be, hmmm?"

Nobody said anything until the judge finished skimming the documents. He wrinkled his forehead suddenly and shook his head. "Ms. Rossi, is this an autopsy report of a hamster? Am I reading this right?"

Nelson covered his mouth to refrain from laughing. I gasped, but of course no one heard me. I couldn't believe she still had it. Mara was unflappable. I stepped closer to her, but not too close.

"The animal was removed from Mr. Andersson's former premises after it died following brief exposure to the chemicals in Mr. Andersson's possession."

"I didn't have anything in my possession that Laney didn't know about." Dipshit Mark couldn't remain quiet any longer. No self-control, as usual. "She was right there with me."

"Counsel, please advise your client of some of those fancy rights of his—and really hit that Fifth Amendment one hard." The judge refocused on Mara. "What kinds of chemicals are we talking about, Ms. Rossi?"

"As you are aware, Your Honor, Mr. Andersson is the creator of SafeLawn. What you might not know is that the product was created outside of a lab, on his own time, in his own house, and tested on his own property, using his wife and child as incidental guinea pigs, all of which is illegal and unethical." She nodded toward the folder the judge held. "You can see per the medical report that the animal died as a result of tumors that replicated themselves at an incredible rate. In the attached picture, you can see the damage to the animal's skin that supports my claim that the creature suffered chemical burns."

"I'm not familiar with the medical terms listed here, Ms. Rossi." The judge looked a little confused.

"Your Honor, this animal was exposed to chemicals outside the former family home for a period of no longer than one hour. I have taken the liberty of forwarding these results to the EPA and FDA, and you can imagine the alarms it sounded, as Mr. Andersson's product is set for mass distribution in the upcoming months."

The judge frowned and stashed the forms back in the folder. "Tell me why I should be taking a man's children away from him."

"I am asking for a custodial review and temporary placement based on these allegations until the FDA and EPA have had a chance to thoroughly review the product in question. Mr. Andersson has access to substantial amounts of this product and is currently testing it around his home and children, despite the fact that it has yet to clear the FDA. Under federal guidelines, Your Honor, that constitutes possession of a controlled substance."

She folded her arms and Nelson scoffed loudly. "You make it sound like he's running a drug lab—like he's some kind of gangster!"

"Playing with anhydrous ammonia? He might as well be." Mara met his astounded glare and didn't waver. "I'm sure the neighbors in that family-friendly association would be interested in knowing about this as well. Furthermore, Ms. Cavallo endured a difficult pregnancy followed by the birth of a son with chronic asthma requiring tens of thousands of dollars for initial and ongoing treatment, a condition likely due to environmental exposure to chemicals in utero or possibly as the result of a transmitted mutated gene due to repeated exposure on the part of his biological father, Mr. Mark Andersson. I've got a collection of compelling case studies that might interest Your Honor."

Nelson's face was a scary shade of red and I wondered what his blood pressure was running long about now. "This is nothing but hokey science! What next—you want to blame my client for the kid falling off his tricycle and scraping his knee because his biological father isn't an avid bike rider? Chrissakes!"

"Nonsense. The only danger I'd be concerned about would be if the child fell off his bike onto a patch of GreenSafe-treated grass."

"I'll do the asking of the questions! This is still my courtroom." The judge slammed his gavel. He aimed it at Mara first, "Let me get a word in, madam." Then he aimed it at Nelson. "And you will refrain from using the Lord's name in vain inside this courtroom!"

The mention of "Lord" from the judge made me a bit nervous. Though in his defense, he didn't seem ruffled when Nelson called Mara my lover in his accusatory voice. I glimpsed at Trinidad, who appeared to be pondering the same things. The action in this courtroom certainly had potential to get interesting.

Nelson was up to bat, again. "This is an outrage. Ms. Rossi doesn't even practice law anymore, Your Honor, and she knows nothing about Florida law."

"And you practiced in New Jersey, Attorney Nelson," she put in. "What experience do you have with this state's law that you'd like to reference?" Mara looked at the judge with all sincerity. "I have a ten-year history in environmental law and its impact on individuals, particularly children and animals. I believe I'm qualified to present myself as the Cavallo-Andersson children's advocate on this matter."

The judge appeared to roll her quick words back through his mind. He must have decided it gelled. Nelson wasn't done yet.

"As my client made crude mention of, Your Honor, Ms. Cavallo was aware of her husband's hobby, thereby calling her own character into question just as much."

Mara responded, "Your Honor, Ms. Cavallo, who can obviously not represent herself at this juncture, did take appropriate action at that time. She removed herself and her daughter from the poisoned premises upon discovering his hobby nearly five years ago. She would have filed an immediate petition for divorce had Mr. Andersson not threatened to keep her 'tied up in court indefinitely' quote-unquote. Mr. Andersson had also previously made threats to kidnap their daughter if Ms. Cavallo attempted to file for a divorce due to his unwillingness to pay child support." She produced more paperwork. "I have handwritten documentation from the deceased dating from the time she left the Andersson household until the day prior to her death. I also have several recorded phone calls leading up to the initial agreement between Mr. Andersson and Ms. Cavallo. Both should substantiate my claims of extortion and terrorism.

And that, Your Honor, should be sufficient grounds to take this issue to trial."

I saw the phone tapes and my private journals before her on the podium. I looked at Trinidad and smiled my thanks to him. He solemnly nodded.

"Give me a break, Your Honor!" Nelson glared at the beautiful opposing counsel. "She's a lesbian unable to have her own children for very obvious biological reasons! Who does she recommend be named temporary custodian? Let me guess— *Mara Rossi?*" He laughed out loud. "Let's stop wasting our time tonight. I'd like to get home to my dinner too."

Nelson gathered his stuff together as if to leave as a display of the opposing counsel's absurdity.

"Who do you recommend, Ms. Rossi? For my own benefit." It was the judge's turn to glare at her.

"I would like to file a motion to have this case moved to New York, and yes, I would like to be granted temporary custody of the Cavallo-Andersson children, as—"

"Big surprise, Your Honor!" Nelson burst out. "There are no grounds for a custody trial—let alone moving the venue to another state! Where did you go to law school, Ms. Rossi?"

"Harvard." Mara answered firmly, refusing to lose patience due to the weight of the subject at hand. "If I can be allowed to continue, there is sufficient evidence on many grounds to explore this further. As I am not eligible to represent the children due to a clear conflict of interest—"

"*Clear* conflict!" Nelson called out.

"Mr. Nelson—one more outburst and you'll be sitting in jail for twenty-four hours. That's my final warning to you."

He looked at Mara with a skepticism that made me uncomfortable. It didn't seem to faze her. "Continue, please. And don't throw a bunch of fancy children's court terminology my way or I'll get bored, fast."

"I am willing to hire an attorney to represent the children's interests based on the court's recommendation. Meanwhile, I request that they be returned immediately to the surroundings they are comfortable in, in New York. I have documentation from the children's school stating their normal record of attendance, as well as a household review and recommendation from DCF of Greater New York. And finally, this." Mara held all the paperwork out for the bailiff. The judge made a "give-me" motion and the man promptly delivered it to him.

The judge took several long minutes to review the material he'd been given. He asked her, "A letter from Justice Lacroix. Impressive."

I had met Aaron Lacroix one time at a dinner at Professor Mills' house. Lacroix had entertained us with stories of a life spent fighting environmental effects upon children and his fight against them. He had a flair for drama, which certainly added to the already-amazing Robin Hood-esque stories that always ended with taking from big business violators and turning over the proceeds to the families they had damaged. Lacroix was one of Professor Mills' dearest friends; a real mover and shaker in DC, and apparently firmly in Mara's corner. Did I mention she's brilliant?

Attorney Nelson gave her his final best glare at the mention of the Supreme Court Justice. At last Judge Timmons finished reviewing Mara's extensive collection of paperwork.

"Your Honor, it's hardly fair that we don't have a copy of anything she's talking about." Nelson again, but his argument was sounding tired.

"You will have every opportunity to review anything you want to when you go to trial." He picked up his gavel, but didn't slam it down just yet. Nelson, meanwhile, did everything but faint.

I was ecstatic.

"On what grounds, Your Honor?" Nelson weakly asked.

"Racketeering will stand. There are one, two...three..." Finally Judge Timmons shook his head. "There's a whole grab bag of possible offenses here. You'll have time to explore it. And I'm granting the change of venue too."

"*What?*" It was Mark, and I was enjoying that he was having a difficult time staying quiet. He looked as if he could crawl right out of his own skin.

"Your *Honor!*" Nelson pleaded.

"It seems that much of this evidence is already on file with the State of New York. I think they can handle it there." Judge Timmons restacked the papers and handed them to his bailiff to make copies.

He turned to Nelson and Mark with a slight grin, his voice low, almost devious. "Oh, you don't want me to try it here in the great State of Florida. I'm a particular fan of a natural environment. I like my surroundings unmanipulated, the way God intended for them to be. And I'm a fan of doing what's right by children. I have six children and eleven grandchildren and I love them all—including the gay one. Trust me, I'm doing you a favor."

Nelson rolled his eyes. He squeaked out a single word. "Custody?"

"These are serious charges with long-term consequences. I'm taking a pass on the restraining order against Mr. Andersson, but I'm ordering the children be surrendered to DCF of New York in one week's time and you will comply. Children and Families there can make the best recommendation for visitation for you," he nodded toward Mark, "and for you, Ms. Rossi, as I believe you both have fundamental roles in the children's upbringing."

Mara closed her eyes and nodded her appreciation. Had I been alive, I surely would have had tears of joy.

"I believe New York will agree that the children deserve their own attorney. Despite the lien I'm placing on your assets, Mr. Andersson, you can pay for that. According to what I see here, you did get off scot-free for nearly five years without paying a cent. Airplane rentals are expensive. So is training to get a pilot's license. You made room for that in your budget, but not your own children? Shame on you."

"I don't understand..." Mark's eyes were like saucers. He looked to Nelson for legal interpretation. He didn't look at Tatum, who'd turned two shades of angry red. "What's happening here? I don't have access to my own money?"

"Incidentally, I'm not a fan of deadbeat dads, either," Judge Timmons declared in his low, Southern voice.

I wondered if he would freak out if I approached the bench and laid a big old invisible kiss on him.

"Thank you, Your Honor." Mara could not hide the relief in her voice.

The gavel slammed and Mark and his clan immediately filed out. Mara coolly put her paperwork into her briefcase and glanced upward at the judge, who was still watching her. She started to leave the courtroom.

"Ms. Rossi." Judge Timmons stopped her. "You've got a hell of an uphill battle where you're headed. I wish I had a better feeling about it. Not every judge is going to feel the same way I do."

She slowly nodded, gave him a little smile. "But it's a start."

Judge Timmons' sturdy countenance was tinged with worry. Mara thanked him and again started out, headed right for me. I quickly moved out of her way, recalling the aura conversation I'd had with Trinidad.

I held my breath as Mara walked right through the place where I'd been standing. The cadence of her smart business shoes slowed and then stopped. She made a slow pivot and looked into my eyes with so much assurance I could swear she actually saw me. Her hesitation bought me time to enjoy her natural beauty, and I couldn't have asked for anything more. Something rose up within me that had every earmark of emotion, and yet I knew that was impossible. Mara was wonderful. She looked absolutely intrigued, as if she were safekeeping a secret. I knew she felt me there.

Unable to break from her gaze, I took two small steps back and stumbled into an antique chair. Its bulky chair legs made a slight screech against the floor upon contact. I didn't dare budge, only stood there, half-leaning in an awkward pose, staring at the love of my life as she stared at…nothing.

"I love you Mara," I whispered anyway. "I do, I do, I do."

Mara smiled, her eyes were gloomy and brilliant at the same time. She emanated a sense of warmth and absolute comfort that permeated me, making me feel light and tingly. I couldn't imagine how a living human could have such an effect on me. I wanted to run to her, hold her close, kiss her senseless. But it was no use. She looked all around me, not quite at me, felt me, but could not see me. The moment lasted seconds but felt like an eternity. She raised my journals and clutched them close to her chest before continuing her exit from the courtroom.

When she was gone, the judge and his bailiff filed out and Trinidad was suddenly behind me. Though my near-fall had not hurt me (as if it could), he gingerly took my elbow and helped me up. I turned to him as the overhead bright fluorescents flickered off and I could see him as clear as the moon in the sky.

"Thank you, Trinidad."

In a robotic move, he nudged me toward him until my cheek rested on his chest. In his attempt at comfort, I experienced some kind of evolution. As he stroked my hair, his cold touch had transmuted and was replaced by the warmth of his beautiful truth. It washed through me in a wave of sadness and joy. I began to cry.

Chapter 32

I lay in Mark and Tatum's guest room late into the night, listening to the quarrelling sounds of the two most selfish adults probably to ever walk the earth. I knew the children were long asleep, and I'd already heard the blond busty nanny creep out hours earlier. I got up and tiptoed down the hallway to peek in on them. I gave the door to Bella's room a little shove and stepped inside.

Lucy was sitting at their bedside reading one of the thick leather-bound volumes she'd borrowed from the study. I considered that on her quest for decent literature, she was probably the only one who would ever actually utilize that room for its intended purpose. It seemed absolutely appropriate that she had selected Brontë's *Jane Eyre*.

I stepped closer and she lowered the book and looked distinctly at me. I froze in place, not daring to move a muscle.

And then she spoke to me.

"They slept like angels right through the excitement, Ms. Cavallo."

I am sure my surprise was obvious. We locked gazes.

"You have very nice children. You must be quite proud."

"I am, thank you."

I studied her sitting there, reading in the dark just as I'd found her many times before. I guess the reading in total darkness-thing should have red-flagged me that Lucy was dead. I felt exposed and realized she probably did too. I shifted my stance, crammed my hands in my burned out pockets and smiled. "Thank you for everything, Lucy. I'm grateful that you're looking after them. It means everything to me."

"I know." She sweetly smiled before returning her attention to her book.

The children were in good, albeit otherworldly, hands. I left them and wandered down the hallway as I pondered things. Judge Timmons was right; Mara had a hell of a fight in front of her. I should have taken the proper steps to divorce my husband and legally redefine my life to better establish Mara's role in the children's lives. Their present miserable situations were my own fault. As a newly Dead, I still had human inclinations, and therefore I'd assigned greater fault to Mark, the greedy son of a bitch who killed me. Asshole-bastard. I'm sure whoever was sponsoring my foray into the living world was probably making extensive notes pertaining to my use of insults and swears, even if only uttered inside my head.

For all the things I might have done in my life without fully engaging my intelligence, not divorcing Mark was certainly at the top of the list. And now he was in charge of raising the children. Poor Mara, who had such a desire, had no rights and had been stripped of all family, forced to watch the children she'd raised as her own relocated to Florida to live in a ridiculous mansion on a patch of poisoned land. It defied everything she stood for concerning her life's work and her fierce sense of protection for our little family.

And finally there were the people, all oblivious to the fact that Mark and his voodoo lawn formula had the power to imbalance the entire ecosystem. I no longer believed that it was a far-fetched statement. One life touches so many; he was going to be "touching" them at an astronomical rate via a mass market retailer. Yeah, I could have hindered that process too.

Trinidad leaned against the wall near the study, and I was surprised to see him out of bed. The man loved to pretend to sleep almost as much as he loved to pretend to eat. I went to him and leaned right next to him.

"Were you there when Mark took the children away from Mara?"

He gave one nod. "She begged him for the children. She offered him a million dollars in exchange. He laughed at her."

I'm sure he figured that was a drop in the bucket compared to what he stood to make. We were quiet for several minutes as we listened to the arguing wind down in the bedroom across the hall. Soon enough, Mark stormed out and disappeared into the guest room, our own usual quarters. I guess Trinidad must have seen that coming.

He smirked softly. "For better or worse. For richer or poorer. In sickness and in health. 'Till death do you part.'" A faint smile played upon his lips. "It occurs to me that you did honor your marriage vows. Not with your husband, but with Mara."

"Yes."

"She loves you very much."

"I know that. I do." I looked away, nearly overcome with emotion again. My senses were gradually refining and improving.

The ticking of the grandfather clock down the hall seemed to amplify and fill the entire second floor with a noise that could serve as either a comfort or a warning. Tonight it felt like the latter. Trinidad sighed and stretched out.

"I'm going to—"

I finished his sentence. "The kitchen, I know."

He grinned at me, and in an uncharacteristic move he aimed his index finger at me and "fired" a shot. I shook my head and watched him go, wondering what I would do with the rest of my night.

The answer was suddenly right in front of me, or rather Mark was. He slipped out of the guest room and strode down the hall, his ridiculously short robe open and flowing behind him like he was some kind of man-diva. I followed him and resisted the temptation to kick the seat of his boxers. Repeatedly.

Inside the study he went straight to his stash hidden in an elaborate cigar box on his desk. He dumped a tiny packet of the stuff on the desk blotter and rummaged in the drawer until he found a tiny plastic ruler, which he used to form a good line. He rolled a Post-It note and snorted the entire line all at once.

"Don't get the sticky part stuck in your nose hairs, dumbass," I muttered.

Mark inhaled deeply and leaned back in his leather throne with his eyes closed.

"So, this is the life, huh?" I sat on the edge of the desk and looked around. "Books you'll never read, children you'll never love…a wife who'll never love you."

Of course. I was a fine one to talk; I had hardly been the ideal wife. Not to him, anyway.

"You couldn't just leave the kids out of this? It's not like you wouldn't have still got the money. Nobody was going to take your goddamn precious money."

His eyes opened and he shook the empty packet. He got up to make himself a drink—scotch and three cubes—and downed it. He made a second before going back to the desk. He clumsily rummaged through the ornate box for another snort, but came up empty. He opened the drawer and rifled around some more, his increasingly jerky movements bordering on desperate, until he found Tatum's little bottle. Pleased with his find, he unscrewed the lid and raised the loaded spoon to his nose.

I leaned on my forearm, practically laying my body across his desk, getting an up-close look at the affluent junkie. His nose was red and so were his eyes. I was close enough to see every pore on his face; closer in proximity than I'd been during most of my married life. I muttered, "Go on and kill those brain cells. You're good at killing things."

He took a few more snorts before leaning back again. He closed his eyes for a good long time, kicked his slippered feet up and rested them on the edge of the desk. He leaned far back in his chair, as far as he could manage without losing balance.

I reached over and picked up the tiny bottle and dangled it in front of his face, but he didn't notice. I set it back down and scooted the things around his desk a little, making myself more comfortable. I snatched a pencil from a metal holder and threw it at him, striking him right on the nose—it was a surefire hit this close up—and when his eyelids sprang open, he looked thoroughly pissed.

Mark looked around, his angry expression replaced by a curious one. He actually closed his eyes again, which I found unusual. I mean if a pencil came flying at me out of nowhere and smacked me in the beezer, I'd at least investigate it. And besides, I was always under the impression that cocaine kept you up and going for days on end, otherwise what's the point of partaking anyway? My own past didn't include dabbling in anything more than maybe an ounce of pot, total, in my life, so I wasn't familiar with the effects beyond anything I'd seen in movies or read about in books. But apparently none of that was true with Mark. His breathing leveled out and his lips parted slightly and then he began his low, throaty snore that I had, thankfully, purged from my memories.

I took the opportunity to look around, checking the drawers that Tatum had been in and out of days earlier, but I wasn't finding much. I became careless about my search, sort of clanging around, but Mark dozed right through it all. I was on a quest for some final piece of incriminating evidence to get to Mara—probably through Trinidad again. I came up empty, which was frustrating.

I was about to give up when I hit pay dirt; a manila folder near the rear of the desk file containing the flimsy faxed facsimiles confirming that the children's life insurance policies had indeed been hiked up to four mil each. I crammed them hastily back into the folder and started for the door with it.

"What the fuck?"

I heard his voice from behind me. I stopped and turned in place and saw Mark looking right through me to what he perceived to be a folder floating across the room. I admit that would have freaked me out too. I had no choice but to drop it and take a step backward. He drunkenly struggled to get out of his chair and stared at the folder for a few seconds. He looked in my direction again and then back to the folder. What a trip. He finally knelt and gathered up the spilled contents and returned with it to the desk. He was fully engrossed in what he was reading, all thoughts of the "floating" folder out the door, and I waited to see what his reaction would be.

"What have we got here?" Mark muttered.

"That's right, dipshit, she's going to off the kids," I said to no one but myself.

He flipped through the paperwork, skimming the details in a relatively uncaring fashion until he came to something that captured his interest above all else. It didn't seem to set well with him. He hunched over and held it closer to the light to get a better look. I crept closer to read over his shoulder and had only barely begun when he raised up again so fast, I nearly didn't have time to get out of the way.

"My insurance policy?" He shook his head. A slow-growing smile emerged on his lips. "You raised my policy, my little harlot? Why, I'm almost proud of you, you silly little bitch."

He laughed and carefully replaced all the paperwork in the folder and dropped it into the bottom drawer. He rooted around the messy desktop until he found the bottle again and hurriedly snorted the remaining coke. He held the jar up and gave it a good look before dropping it into his robe pocket and then he was off. I practically had to run to keep up with him.

I followed him through the dark mansion, downstairs, and outside, all the way across the lawn until we came to the little shed. He entered and felt blindly in the darkness until he was able to find and yank the string on the swinging light fixture. Yellow light bathed the place and he went straight to a stack of GreenSafe bags. From his robe pocket he pulled out the jar and the pocketknife he'd carried for as long as I'd known him. It had been his grandfather's knife and had a pearl handle with a monogram etched on it and a little groove in the casing. I'd nearly blocked out an incident of having seen it up close before. Boy, as a Dead, even the most suppressed memories are right there on the surface in high-definition.

He plunged the knife into the bag on top and yanked it back

a couple of inches, exposing the poison lawn fertilizer. With as much grace as his trembling hands would permit, he filled Tatum's tiny red jar to capacity, recapped it and blew away the excess.

"I may be worth four mil, but you're worth an impressive six," he muttered, chuckling. "So who's got the last laugh now, baby? Kill me and my kids? Think again, bitch."

Nothing—not the hyperinflated insurance policies or even him replacing Tatum's coke—*nothing* could have surprised me more than hearing him take any kind of stand on the children's behalf, twisted and sick as the situation was. As he stormed out of the shed and back toward the house, my fear and respect for Mark peaked simultaneously. I didn't know whether to—or even *how* to—intervene in his planning, and it could only end badly.

Chapter 33

Four years, eleven months, three days and two hours before I died.
Cooper Rossi Cavallo was born September 25th at 5:55 p.m.
He was a little guy, a whopping six pounds even, and almost
immediately he was whisked away to neonatal intensive care.

My labor had lasted nearly forty hours and I was completely
worn out. Mara had been an excellent coach and comfort, and
she did her best to allay my fears about my newborn son's health.
I insisted to her that I would be fine; that she should follow
the baby to the NICU. I barely even remember her leaving my
room before I fell asleep.

At nearly two a.m., I awoke to find her asleep in the chair
she'd pushed as close to the bed as she could possibly get. Her
hand was lying loosely inside mine and I gave it a soft squeeze.
She startled awake and her eyelashes fluttered. She stretched
her arms and leaned over to kiss my forehead.

"How's the baby?" I asked.

"He's beautiful," she said, sweeping her fingers through my messy hair. I felt like I'd been through the wringer, probably looked equally scary.

"They took him away so quickly…"

Mara's expression turned serious. "His breathing was a little muddy, so they gave him oxygen. But they said that's pretty common. Remember that the kid took his own sweet time getting here, you know?"

"How could I forget?" I grimaced at the memory. Still, I felt worried. "You're sure he's good?"

She nodded, but had a troubled look about her.

"What is it?"

"I've been thinking about it and I think we should hyphenate Cooper's last name," she said at last. "I know how you feel about him not having anything to do with Mark, but we should at least consider putting his name on the birth certificate."

I started to argue the point before I remembered that one of the reasons I loved Mara was because she was brilliant. "State your case, counselor."

"Legally, you can name a child whatever you want. Mark could protest it, but he doesn't even know about Cooper, so you're probably fine there. Psychologically speaking, don't you think the children should have the same last name? We want them to feel connected and secure."

"Psychologically speaking—mine and theirs…" I paused, felt weepy all the sudden. "I'd like us to all have your last name."

She flashed a sympathetic smile and smoothed my hair. "I know sweetie. But you're legally married and you'd need Mark's permission to change Bella's name. There's no way he'd go for that."

"I know."

"For medical purposes we have to at least list him as the father. If anything should happen—God forbid Cooper should need a transplant or a transfusion or what have you, he should have some evidence that he's Mark's biological son."

She waited for my reaction, but I was still thinking it through when she added, "And he is the father and we know that. Your mom would say that's a lie of omission." Her face was lit only by the glow of the nightlight.

I nodded at last. "Cooper Rossi Cavallo-Andersson," I rolled the name around.

"Kid's going to need a tutor in kindergarten just to learn to spell all that."

We laughed quietly.

"You think it's the right thing to do?" I asked her.

"It is," she whispered. "And it's important to do the right thing. Everything counts, Laney."

I finally verbalized something that had been bothering me since discovering I was pregnant. "Do you think Cooper will be anything at all like Mark?" Almost involuntarily I covered my mouth, and tearfully added, "That would really kill me."

"Ah, the old argument—nature versus nurture." She sounded as if she were reciting an ancient Chinese proverb. Her smile was genuine and she clasped my hand tightly. "With us around? My money's on nurture. Lots and lots and lots of nurture."

"Mine, too," I told her, smiling.

Mara buzzed the nurse and asked her to bring Cooper into the room. A short while later he joined us, free of oxygen or any devices, looking like he was completely blameless for my nervous pregnancy or his lackadaisical style of entering the world. He looked tiny and sweet and pink-faced, and I loved him. The nurse wheeled his cart to the bedside and left us. We stared at the sleeping baby for a bit until I told her what I knew she was dying to hear. "Go on. What are you waiting for?"

Mara bit her lip, looked rather unsure of herself as she lifted the baby from the clear bin. Jostling him a bit, she settled in right next to me in the little bed. She raised her knees up like a teepee and leaned them against mine and rested Cooper there. We quietly poked and prodded him, counting toes and playing with wispy white hair. He slept on, oblivious to our doting.

"He's beautiful, Laney. He's the most beautiful boy I've ever seen." Her voice was scratchy and rich with emotion.

I lay my head on her shoulder and nestled in tight. I knew Cooper couldn't have lucked into more love if he'd tried. Sturdy love, that's what we had. I felt it clear through to my bones. Real tug-at-the-heart, butterflies-in-the-belly, long lasting, stars-in-your-eyes love. Nature be damned, nurture had it hands down.

Mara kissed my forehead. She spoke as if she were reading my very thoughts.

"It's a good life we have, Laney. A really charmed, good life."

Chapter 34

At nearly eight, the sound of Tatum's voice awoke everyone for as many mornings in a row, but for a change she wasn't screaming or ranting. I figured I was low on time and had spent the night in Bella's room, firmly wedged between both children. I carefully rearranged them as I sat up and looked over at Trinidad, who'd been asleep in the chair. We both regarded each other with a bit of mystery about the trilling voice from below. Tatum was calling everyone to breakfast.

"Oh..." Bella was the first to register a complaint as I rousted them awake. They got out of bed and I chased them around with clothes and oversaw the tooth-brushing festivities. They were ready inside of five minutes, some sort of kid land-record. They hit the hallway the same time Tatum's voice sounded again from downstairs.

We followed the children to the kitchen, where to my great

surprise Tatum was manning the stove herself. No other staff was present. Trinidad and I exchanged puzzled expressions.

"To the table you two, hurry, hurry!"

Tatum shepherded Bella and Cooper over to the table where their places had been set. She fairly clumsily scooped eggs onto plates next to bacon.

"Now, I'm getting the toast too. So, hold your horses."

Mark entered the room at that moment, and not even the Deads in the room could trump his level of surprise. Or suspicion.

"Where's the cook?"

"Morning off, which is fine. It's been a long time since I've cooked anything in my own kitchen."

"You've never cooked anything in your own kitchen. What gives?"

"Don't be ridiculous." She arched a perfectly manicured eyebrow and held up a spatula with eggs on it, issued a forced southern "Sit yourself down. I'll serve you up."

Mark chuckled, asked, "What? Is there a magazine reporter milling around somewhere this morning?"

"Now why would you ask me a thing like that?" She plunged four slices of bread into an industrial quality toaster and then stood by, fussing with the tie of an apron that was too big for her—the strings wrapped around her twice. Tatum cast a glance over Mark's shoulder at the children who were watching with silent, growing interest. "Go on now, eat up."

Mark remained staring at her, but raised a halting hand toward the table. "No kids. Not so fast."

Tatum practically batted her eyelashes. "Now why on earth can't they? It'll get cold if they don't—"

"Because I said," he practically growled the words. He nodded toward the lunches already packed and waiting on the countertop. "You make those too?"

"Well they weren't going to make themselves." She thrust her hands on her tiny hips and looked more than a little dismayed. "What the hell has gotten into you?"

Mark stared at her as he sauntered toward the table where the children sat. He took both plates laid out before them and dumped them—plate and all—into the garbage pail. He raised his hands in a show of defiance. Tatum's cheeks burned with obvious fury. Mark turned around and dug his wallet out of his wrinkled jeans.

"Bell, Coop, you get lunch at school today, you hear?" He handed a few bills to Bella. "You're in charge of that; you can handle a thing like that, right?"

Bella nodded eagerly. He petted her head like a dog, but it was an effort. "Good girl. Okay, everybody grab a backpack and get on out of here. Driver's waiting."

The pair scrambled down from their places and were out the door in a flash. My eyes followed them, and I wished I could have said goodbye, but I admit I was interested to see what fireworks were brewing in that kitchen. I glanced at Trinidad and saw that he was similarly captivated.

Tatum angrily began dumping the untouched food still on the platters into the garbage. Nobody bothered to fetch the discarded plates. Mark leaned against the counter, his tone blasé. "Poisoning apples are we, wicked stepmother?"

She whirled around and jammed her finger into his chest. "Listen here you miserable son of a bitch! I have made everything possible for you, do you hear me? *Everything!* What would make you think such a fucked-up thing?"

He grabbed her jabbing finger and held it tight in midair. They stood there, nose to nose, not more than a breath between them.

Mark smirked, said in a menacingly low, gravelly voice, "Because I've considered doing it to you so many times myself." His eyes went momentarily and alarmingly wide. Then he laughed and lowered his chin. "Like anyone's buying that good-mother routine."

"Oh! Get over yourself!" she bellowed, sans the accent.

He remained staring at her for several seconds, then released her finger, turned on his heel and marched out of the kitchen.

Furious, Tatum threw the skillet. The remaining food went flying before it clattered to the floor. She stalked after him.

We followed the simmering madness, which came to a boil in the study.

Mark leaned against the oversized desk. He held the manila folder from the night before and slapped it against his opposite hand in a slow, steady rhythm. The action didn't even pique Tatum's interest; she was more focused on her anger. She slammed the door shut and continued her lecture.

"Don't take your pissy behavior out on me—I didn't file a motion to take those fucking kids away from you! I did everything to help you get those rugrats! I will not have you taking it out on me!"

He waved the folder, smiled. "Yes, I can see that you have my best interests at heart."

Recognition shone in her eyes and she swallowed hard. "What? Of course I do! As soon as I get the notification about the EPA and FDA putting a hold on GreenSafe—"

"Wait a minute." He squinted. "You knew about them opening an investigation?"

"Well of course I did—I am the heart and soul of this operation," she spat. "As soon as I found out I had to make sure there was a backup plan."

"And doing in the kids for insurance money was the perfect plan, huh?"

She blinked several times, her voice soft. "Well, it wasn't a perfect plan. I just wanted us to have…options." She appeared to consider it and smugly smiled. "This coming from the man who killed his own wife for money—you picked a hell of a time to develop a conscience, darling."

Mark approached her, waved the folder again, his voice low and steady. "You gonna do me in too?" He chuckled. "Was that one of your options?"

"What?" She faked a good perplexed look. Tatum lowered her eyes and her voice. "Darling, I don't do the killing. That's your department."

He set the folder behind him on the desk and kept moving slowly toward her.

"Was someone else going to take care of it for you? Because it occurs that without me you'd have no henchman to take care of your dirty work."

"Bullshit! Don't act with me like I ordered you to crash that fucking plane! That was you—all *you!*"

"Well, then maybe you wanna tell me how my love became more valuable overnight?" He waved the insurance policy. "I admit I'm a hell of a lay, but four million might be pushing it."

"Oh, that *would* be pushing it!" she hissed. "If you must know, I raised your insurance policy up too so that increasing theirs didn't look obvious, jackass."

"And who, pray tell, authorized these changes?" He seemed downright amused. "Let me guess—me, right? The old signature switcheroo just like we did with my dearly departed wife?"

Tatum didn't move a muscle. Mark's head bobbed.

"That's what I figured. You are one clever girl, I gotta hand it to you. You left no stone unturned."

"Marcus, I am only looking out for you. God knows somebody has to." Her stance suddenly softened, and she took a step closer to him, smiled and gently raked her hands through his hair. She leaned into him until their noses were touching, whispered, "I did it for you. For us."

I watched them as they kissed, tentatively at first, then more deeply. After a few minutes, he kissed a path to her ear, whispered, "I really can only thank you."

"I've got your back," she purred. She held him close, stood on tiptoe to put her chin against his shoulder, whispered sexily into his ear. "You need me. No offense, darling, but you are a teensy bit of a fuck-up."

Mark's eyes hardened and in one swift move, he jerked her back and unwound the apron from around her waist. It was around Tatum's neck before she could process it. He pulled it tight until she made a strained whimper, but nothing more. Her eyes were horrifically wide and she batted her hands at him, but he held her out from him, tsking at her wasted effort. She swung and swatted uselessly, practically spinning in place. Mark yanked the strings in the opposite direction until her body jerked. Blood infiltrated her eyes like streaks of red lightning.

Instinctively, I started toward them, but Trinidad grabbed my arm and pulled me back to him.

"You cannot interfere."

I looked at him aghast. "He's going to kill her! We can't just stand by and do nothing!"

He coolly shook his head. "Rules."

I wondered how it could be that I could be brought back from...wherever, to save my children—to save the *world*, possibly, and yet we were going to stand by and watch a woman be murdered. I moved my arms behind my back and clamped my hands tightly onto the edge of the desk, physically holding myself in place.

Mark throttled her. Her feet struggled for floor, but she was losing the battle.

"I'm stronger than you, Tatie. I mean, you were going to die—I just didn't know it was going to be today, at this exact minute. But I'm a flexible guy. I'll roll with it," he hissed through gritted teeth. "But I owe you a debt of gratitude. Since yours is the only policy that wasn't all jacked up recently, makes me look real good."

He grimaced, breathless, taking sick pleasure in spelling out for her just what he was doing as she struggled.

"I'll stage a little robbery. That kitchen scuffle back there will help. Luckily I had you insured to the hilt long ago."

Tatum went limp and Mark coldly dropped her body. It landed on the floor with a weighty thud. We watched as he swiveled her diamond ring over her knuckle and pocketed it.

Then Mark went about the room cleaning up. He crammed the insurance paperwork back into the drawer and noticed his glass with its melted ice still perched on the desktop, left over from last night. He opened the liquor cabinet and poured new right in over the old and raised it in a toast.

"Never fuck with a guy who watches C.S.I." He tossed the drink back and slammed it down with a satisfied smile. He poured himself another, but didn't touch it just yet. Instead he picked up the phone, his expression turning serious, and pressed 911. In moments he was wailing into the receiver. "Help me! It's my wife! Something's happened to my wife! My God, my God...!"

He was effective with his tears, and even from the great beyond the performance gave me the chills. I looked at Trinidad, who was checking his watch. The sand had almost run out; I didn't know what that meant.

"No! No! Nobody else is here…oh God! I have to go *help her!* CPR or something! I have to help her!" Mark sobbed loudly and then slammed the phone back in the cradle. He swiped his hand across his nose and went back for his drink, downing the second one with the same gusto as the first.

He snarled, "You should have known better than to mess with me."

He took the glass and rooted around the drawer until he found Tatum's stash.

"No need to sound any alarms now, huh?" He went toward the door, stopped and surveyed his wake. His eyes were wild as if he'd lapsed into full-fledged insanity. "Fuck with the bull and you'll get the horn every time, my love. Every time."

He addressed her as if she were merely sleeping, unconsciously uncapping the bottle as he did so. He didn't remember refilling the little bottle with GreenSafe? Could he actually be so inebriated?

"No!" I screamed to deaf living ears. "No! Don't do it!"

He stuck a full spoon to his nose and snorted.

Mark shuddered, looked stunned. His smile faded. Beads of sweat formed on his forehead and he pulled the bottle back for inspection. He wore an expression of sheer disbelief as he realized what he'd done.

"Oh…shit."

Chapter 35

Being in the ICU of Palm Hospital was a disconcerting experience for me. Newly Deads cruised past me, as if they were in a hurry to get to some big party in the afterlife. Others wandered around as if they had no better place to be. I stood at Mark's bedside, watching as every monitor blipped and beeped. I was never so glad to see anyone as I was Trinidad when he finally appeared on the other side of the glass door. He weaved around two nurses jamming up the narrow quarters until he reached me.

"She's alive."

"How the hell...?" I shook my head. "You knew that at the house, didn't you?"

He shrugged. "Rules." He looked at Mark and seemed concerned about his situation.

"But Mark is going to die, isn't he?"

Trinidad didn't answer that. Instead he said, "His attorney is on his way up here."

I watched Mark's eyelids flutter. He'd slipped in and out of consciousness all morning. "I need a minute," I murmured.

He stepped back and leaned against the glass wall. I knew there was no danger that the nurses would hear me. Still, I sat on the side of the bed and leaned over Mark. I studied his pasty skin and blue-tinted lips. Dark circles underscored his eyes. I shook my head.

"What a waste of a life," I muttered. I stooped over and rested my chin on my hand, trying to figure out where to start, wondering if it was already too late.

"What a waste of my life too," I added. "Everything's ruined."

The covers beneath me shifted and I watched as Mark struggled to open his eyes. When he did, he looked right through me, or so I thought. He wrinkled his nose and parted his lips, but no words came out. He looked horrified. I was struck with nervousness.

"Can you see me?" I sat up a little straighter. His eyes widened as his answer. I glanced over at the monitor, which showed a dull, thready heartbeat, so I knew he was still technically alive. "Can you hear me?"

Oblivious to the patient's waking state, the nurses exited.

"You...?" He looked scared, but I didn't have time to field his inquiries. I knew if he could see me he wasn't long for this world.

"Listen to me. You have to tell them to send the kids back to Mara." I grasped the material of his flimsy hospital gown. "Do you understand me? You have to."

"To...?" He stammered and blinked.

"Listen to me!" I tightened my hold. "If you don't send the kids back to Mara, they're going to shuffle them around through the legal system—possibly for years! You can do this one thing right."

He gave my ruined clothes the once-over. "Look at you..."

"Nelson is on his way up here—you've got to tell him to send the kids back to Mara."

"I can't, I can't..."

"You can! You can, you miserable son of a bitch! It's the least you can do for them! You've already robbed them of their mother!" I was shaking his bedclothes now, my anxiousness making itself known better than ever before. The monitor showed sudden exaggerated peaks and valleys in his heart rhythm. "Give them back to Mara—for chrissakes!"

I felt Trinidad's hand on my shoulder and knew that I needed to calm down. I wanted to scream and cry. I felt my breathing increase and my chest actually felt tight. My yelling segued into pleading. "Please, please I beg of you. Do this last thing for the children. For once in your life do the right thing, please."

His eyes welled and tears spilled across his cheeks. "I'm... dying."

And I realized how horrifying that realization must have been for him. At least with me, I died instantly with no real time to mull over my pending doom, except for the seconds it took for the plane to crash. Mark was taking the slow path to death, but he was definitely taking it, evidenced by the fact that we were even having a conversation.

I felt something within me change; a slow-growing feeling of empathy for the man who'd robbed me of my life. I brushed his hair away from his face and smiled, felt my breath catch in my throat. I whispered, "It's going to be okay."

His lips moved for several seconds before any sound emerged. His tears flowed freely. "I don't want to die. I...don't want to die."

I offered him every maternal consolation I could conjure up. "It's okay. You won't be in pain. I promise."

"I crashed...on purpose."

"I know."

"I didn't really want you dead."

What could I say? I knew it was the closest thing to a sincere apology I'd ever get from Mark. I felt dizzy with indefinable emotion, and I knew I owed him an apology as well. "I'm sorry you didn't know about our son. That wasn't right."

He closed his eyes and I thought he was fading again. At last he spoke. "He's a good boy. They're both good."

"Yes, they are. And that's why we have to do what's right." I stroked his stubbly, tear-soaked cheek. "You have to tell Nelson to give the kids back to Mara. It's the right thing to do. She loves them very much, Mark. She would lay down her life for them."

He began to sob. "I don't want to die...I don't want to...!"

"Nelson's on his way in." Trinidad again. My companion walked around to the other side of Mark's bed.

I glanced through the glass and saw the lawyer checking in with the ward clerk. He lumbered our direction but was intercepted by a doctor just outside the door. From the look on Nelson's face, the doctor was being candid about Mark's prognosis.

"Please Mark! We've got no time. You've got to tell them!"

He shook his head, confined by the oxygen tubes taped to his nose. His monitor began to beep loudly. The doctor's head swiveled toward us. I felt my body lurch.

"Please! Please Mark!"

The doctor pushed through the door followed by Nelson. Mark's eyes were glassy, he was dying. I felt nauseous.

"Mark, can you hear me?" Nelson leaned across me. "Buddy, can you hear me?"

The doctor checked the monitor and pressed his fingertips to Mark's neck, feeling for a pulse. Trinidad laid a hand on Mark's shoulder. It was as if a jolt passed through him. The monitor leveled off, the beeps settled down and Mark blinked and focused in on Nelson. The heavyset attorney smiled a sad but genuine smile and I was glad to realize that Mark's probably only friend was at his bedside for his passing. It made me miss Mara dreadfully, but I had to put that out of my mind, had to focus on my objective.

I whispered, "Give the children back, Mark. Make it right."

He glanced at me and then back to the attorney. His eyes welled again and he cried silently for a while as Nelson patted his shoulder. The poor old guy was getting jammed up. I felt incredibly faint and lay my head down on the bed for a moment. Then I heard it.

"Send the kids to New York. Send them to..." He closed his eyes again.

I nudged him, prompted, "Send them to Mara Rossi."

Nelson was straining to hear his client and friend. "I want to make sure I understand what you're saying, buddy."

"Send the kids to…Rossi. You have to do that for me."

I squeezed Mark's hand and Nelson's eyes widened. Then he said something that I had not considered. "The children will go to your family."

Mark rolled his head from side to side, dislodging the tubes from his nose. "Not my family. Not my family…to Rossi."

Nelson looked thoroughly confused. "I can't be sure you know what you're saying, Mark. *Mara Rossi?*" He shook his head. "Surely your family will contest that. And you're…not in your sound mind, old pal."

Mark made a weak grab at Nelson's sleeve. He pulled the man down toward him. "You know how to fix it. You know how to fix it."

Nelson shot a look toward the doctor, who was still fussing about. The doctor pretended not to hear.

"Fix it! Promise me."

At last Nelson nodded. "I can fix it." He patted his friend's chest. "I'll take care of it if you're sure that's absolutely what you want."

Mark nodded. He closed his eyes. I closed mine too as the room began to spin.

"I killed my wife."

My eyes sprang open again and I inventoried the expressions on the faces of the doctor and the lawyer. The doctor was far more surprised than Nelson.

"Okay. All right." Nelson patted him again. He leaned over and pressed a kiss onto Mark's forehead. He pulled a hankie from his jacket pocket and dabbed at his eyes, clearly losing his battle with emotion. Mark clenched his friend's arm, but Nelson gently shrugged off his touch, looking ashamed of himself. "I'm sorry, old friend, but I can't stay. I can't watch…"

"No!" Mark cried. "The kids!"

Tears fell from Nelson's eyes and he smiled. "It's been a good run, old friend. A hell of a good run."

He gently shoved Mark's hand away and apologized to the doctor before making his exit. Mark cried silently and the machine began to beep again. He struggled to stay awake, to stay alive. I felt myself fading and climbed onto the bed next to him. I took his hands and smiled.

"Laney…"

"I'm here, Mark. Don't be afraid. Don't be afraid."

I was drifting, falling someplace. I heard the sound of the doctor and nurse as they converged upon us and I tried to reach for Trinidad; tried to call out to him. My companion's gentle face held nothing but peace. He smiled at me as I fell further away into a slow-moving tornado of my life's story. I saw my precious Bella on her first day of preschool. I heard the tiny sound of Cooper's newborn cry. I saw Mara and was grateful to once again look into the eyes of the most beautiful person and caring lover that I'd ever had the privilege of loving.

"Stand clear!" The doctor's voice penetrated the chaos unwinding within me. A blinding white light jolted me and I struggled to see past it at who was standing behind it, but I could not. The last of the sand sifted through the hourglass. Warm fingers clasped my hand and pulled me gently, yet forcefully, toward the brilliance. I was not afraid.

A second jolt struck me and I let go. I felt the life go from me once again as I plunged into blackness.

Epilogue

The sun was high overhead and warm on my face. I blinked against its incredible brightness and surveyed my surroundings as the noise of the city slowly came up around me. I was on a sidewalk across the street from my children's school in the West Village. I was walking and I was not alone.

"I am dead."

The words were spoken by a disheveled mid-thirties gentleman wearing jeans and a torn plaid flannel shirt who walked beside me. He had one arm.

"What makes you say that?" I asked him, looking for the first time at my own clothing. I wore jeans and my favorite cream cowl neck sweater under a denim jacket. I wore shoes. The air felt cool. I could *feel.* I tightened my jacket around me and shoved my hands into the pockets.

"Because everybody's wearing coats, and yet I don't feel

cold."

"What do you feel?"

"Kind of warm, I guess." He shrugged the shoulder of his one good arm. "I feel like I should be more worried that my arm is gone, but I'm not. It's not painful. I can't feel anything." He paused, looked thoroughly bewildered. "Who are you?"

I studied him momentarily. "I'm Laney."

"Who are you to me?"

"I'm…your companion." I smiled reassuringly at him. I knew his name was Luis. I knew a lot of things. "It's better than coming through alone. You have questions."

He looked around him, but I was busy studying a woman with two children walking far ahead of us. She held their hands, swinging them as they went. The little girl also held tight to a leash, and at the end of it a small white dog proudly led the way. I swallowed hard and prompted a quicker pace from my companion as we walked on.

"Hey, I know this place," Luis said. His voice contained an element of wonderment.

"Do you now?"

"Yeah. My family ran a little store a few blocks that way on Tenth and West. Lived in an apartment over it." He grew quiet. Then said, "My mom still lives there. I haven't seen her in a long time."

The breeze carried the smell of flowers from a newsstand across the street. The vendor scampered around, placing bricks on his papers to keep them from being whisked away in the wind. A leftover *Sunday Times* book review blew along the sidewalk, and with near x-ray precision I read the headline.

NY Professor Writing Tell-All About GreenSafe Scandal.

Professor Mills finally decided to pick up a pen.

We came to a corner and stopped for the after-school traffic. I watched the little family step onto the curb across the street and keep going. Suddenly the dog yanked the leash from the little girl's grip. The animal did an about-face and ran in full four-legged steam toward the stream of traffic. In a flash, the little boy peeled his hand away and gave chase. The girl dashed after them both. I stepped away from my companion as the kids and dog bounded toward the opposite corner, fast approaching the busy street.

My beautiful children.

I raised my hand in an automatic halting motion as I'd once seen Trinidad do. McDuff-the-dog—no longer a puppy—came to a screeching stop at the corner. He stared at me, tail wagging, as the kids caught up with him.

"How'd you do that?" Luis was amazed. "Are you an angel?"

I smiled, never removing my gaze from the children. "Far from it."

Cooper followed the dog's line of sight until he saw me. He jumped and waved and yelled hello. I smiled and gave him a little wave. Bella looked through traffic, straining to see the target of her brother's antics. I waved at her for a long time, but she was now too grown up to see me. She was a year older, taller and more beautiful than I could have imagined. I heard her softly chastising my son as she took him by the hand and led him back to Mara. Back to their mother.

Mara gently scooped Cooper up and into her arms and playfully patted his rear end. That quickly, he'd forgotten about seeing me. He threw his head back and dissolved into a fit of giggles as they continued their route home.

My head filled with sweet music and my chest overflowed with a love that was too powerful. I felt pain and joy—I felt everything. I watched them go until they were out of sight. Never could I have loved three people and one goofy dog more.

"Do you have the answers to my questions?"

I glanced at the shifting sands on my three-dimensional wristwatch and knew there was much to do. I turned to Luis, recognized his struggle, and then I smiled.

"No. You do."

**Publications from
Bella Books, Inc.**
The best in contemporary lesbian fiction

**P.O. Box 10543, Tallahassee, FL 32302
Phone: 800-729-4992
www.bellabooks.com**

CALM BEFORE THE STORM by Peggy J. Herring. Colonel Marcel Robideaux doesn't tell and so far no one official has asked, but the amorous pursuit by Jordan McGowan has her worried for both her career and her honor.
978-0-9677753-1-9 $12.95

THE WILD ONE by Lyn Denison. Rachel Weston is busy keeping home and head together after the death of her husband. Her kids need her and what she doesn't need is the confusion that Quinn Farrelly creates in her body and heart.
978-1-931513-65-4 $12.95

LESSONS IN MURDER by Claire McNab. There's a corpse in the school with a neat hole in the head and a Black & Decker drill alongside. Which teacher should Inspector Carol Ashton suspect? Unfortunately, the alluring Sybil Quade is at the top of the list. First in this highly lauded series.
978-1-931513-65-4 $12.95

WHEN AN ECHO RETURNS by Linda Kay Silva. The bayou where Echo Branson found her sanity has been swept clean by a hurricane—or at least they thought. Then an evil washed up by the storm comes looking for them all, one-by-one. Second in series.
978-1-59493-225-0 $14.95

FAÇADES by Alex Marcoux. Everything Anastasia ever wanted—she has it. Sidney is the woman who helped her get it. But keeping it will require a price—the unnamed passion that simmers between them.
978-1-59493-239-7 $14.95

WHISPERS IN THE WIND by Frankie J. Jones. It began as a camping trip, then a simple hike. Dixon Hayes and Elizabeth Colter uncover an intriguing cave on their hike, changing their world, perhaps irrevocably.
978-1-59493-037-9 $12.95

SUBSTITUTE FOR LOVE by Karin Kallmaker. No substitutes, ever again! But then Holly's heart, body and soul are captured by Reyna... Reyna with no last name and a secret life that hides a terrible bargain, one written in family blood.
978-1-931513-62-3 $14.95

MAKING UP FOR LOST TIME by Karin Kallmaker. Take one Next Home Network Star and add one Little White Lie to equal mayhem in little Mendocino and a recipe for sizzling romance. This lighthearted, steamy story is a feast for the senses in a kitchen that is way too hot.
978-1-931513-61-6 $14.95

HUNTING THE WITCH by Ellen Hart. The woman she loves—used to love—offers her help, and Jane Lawless finds it hard to say no. She needs TLC for recent injuries and who better than a doctor? But Julia's jittery demeanor awakens Jane's curiosity. And Jane has never been able to resist a mystery. Number 9 in series and Lammy-winner.
 978-1-59493-206-9 $15.95

WILDFIRE by Lynn James. From the moment botanist Devon McKinney meets ranger Elaine Thomas the chemistry is undeniable. Sharing—and protecting—a mountain for the length of their short assignments leads to unexpected passion in this sizzling romance by newcomer Lynn James.
978-1-59493-191-8 $14.95

DEADLY INTERSECTIONS by Ann Roberts. Everyone is lying, including her own father and her girlfriend. Leaving matters to the professionals is supposed to be easier! Third in series with *PAID IN FULL* and *WHITE OFFERINGS.*
978-1-59493-224-3 $14.95

ELENA UNDONE by Nicole Conn. The risks. The passion. The devastating choices. The ultimate rewards. Nicole Conn rocked the lesbian cinema world with *Claire of the Moon* and has rocked it again with *Elena Undone*. This is the book that tells it all...
978-1-59493-254-0 $16.95

WEDDING BELL BLUES by Julia Watts. She'll do anything to save what's left of her family. Anything. It didn't seem like a bad plan...at first. Hailed by readers as Lammy-winner Julia Watts' funniest novel.
978-1-59493-199-4 $12.95

2ND FIDDLE by Kate Calloway. Cassidy James's first case left her with a broken heart. At least this new case is fighting the good fight, and she can throw all her passion and energy into it.
978-1-59493-200-7 $12.95

LEAVING L.A. by Kate Christie. Eleanor Chapin is on the way to the rest of her life when Tessa Flanagan offers her a lucrative summer job caring for Tessa's daughter Laya. It's only temporary and everyone expects Eleanor to be leaving L.A...
978-1-59493-221-2 $14.95

SOMETHING TO BELIEVE by Robbi McCoy. When Lauren and Cassie meet on a once-in-a-lifetime river journey through China their feelings are innocent...at first. Ten years later, nothing—and everything—has changed. From Golden Crown winner Robbi McCoy.
978-1-59493-214-4 $14.95

DEVIL'S ROCK: THE SEARCH FOR PATRICK DOE by Gerri Hill. Deputy Andrea Sullivan and Agent Cameron Ross vow to bring a killer to justice. The killer has other plans. Gerri Hill pens another intriguing blend of mystery and romance in this page-turning thriller.
978-1-59493-218-2 $14.95

SHADOW POINT by Amy Briant. Madison Maguire has just been not-quite fired, told her brother is dead and discovered she has to pick up a five-year-old niece she's never met. After she makes it to Shadow Point it seems like someone—or something—doesn't want her to leave. Romance sizzles in this ghost story from Amy Briant.
978-1-59493-216-8 $14.95

JUKEBOX by Gina Daggett. Debutantes in love. With each other. Two young women chafe at the constraints of parents and society with a friendship that could be more, if they can break free. Gina Daggett is best known as "Lipstick" of the columnist duo Lipstick & Dipstick.
978-1-59493-212-0 $14.95

BLIND BET by Tracey Richardson. The stakes are high when Ellen Turcotte and Courtney Langford meet at the blackjack tables. Lady Luck has been smiling on Courtney, but Ellen is a wild card she may not be able to handle.
978-1-59493-211-3 $14.95